THE ABRACADABRA CADAVER

A Hillbilly Hexes Cozy Mystery

ELLIE MOSES

Copyright © 2020 by Ellie Moses

All rights reserved.

No part of this book may be reproduced in any form or by any electronic or mechanical means, including information storage and retrieval systems, without written permission from the author, except for the use of brief quotations in a book review.

1

I wandered through the backyard of Genie and Billy Jack's brand new bed, breakfast and brewery over in Cumberland Gap with my hand firmly in Ray's incorporeal one. The place was being christened with the wedding of Granny Mack and Mr. B and boy howdy, was it the prettiest sight I'd seen in a month of Sundays!

A freshly painted white gazebo draped in the royal purple bunting of the Seelie Court, with pots of lilacs spread all around, was the center of attention and the perfect setting for the bride and groom to take their vows. I knew the lilacs had been a house-warming gift to Genie from Granny Mack herself. Their sweet scent permeated the area and I was pleased that my magical kinfolk had pulled out all the stops to make this night something extra special.

"Reminds me of the colors you wanted for our wedding," Ray said as he touched some violets on one of the supper tables that ringed the area. Every purple flower in the state seemed to rest right here in the simple, yet exquisitely romantic setting where my granny would finally marry the man of her dreams.

"I guess Granny's love of purple rubbed off on me over the years." I murmured as I swallowed the lump that had formed in my throat.

Ray's mention of our wedding, that we'd never had due to his untimely demise, tugged the corners of my mouth into a frown. I sighed in resignation as I looked overhead, admiring the lighting above. Garlands of twinkling lights, strung from the limbs of the ancient oak trees that dotted the property, illuminated the area with a soft glow.

Uncle Joe's band from out of Flat Lick, The Shifty River Boys, which was comprised of three of his old high school friends that were also wolf shifters, was setting up beside the gazebo on the stage. Billy Jack had built it right after he and Genie signed the closing papers on the place in anticipation of providing live entertainment every Friday night to promote the brewery part of the business.

I was fixing to go inside and compliment Genie on the ambience when a loud man in a purple vest and white, frilly shirt came barreling past me and Ray.

His face was nearly as purple as the bunting hanging from the gazebo and he glared back over his shoulder.

"Sugar, wait!" A cute blonde called out as she brushed past in his wake, her voice pleading reason. By the look of things, I knew this must not be the first time she'd chased after him hoping to lighten his thunderous mood. I wondered who they were since I didn't recognize either one of them.

To her credit, she wore the prettiest dress I'd seen in a long while. It was short enough to show off her tanned legs and it dazzled the eye even in the low light with purple sequins and a fringed hem that put me in mind of the flapper dresses of the 1920s.

"Must be a lover's spat," Ray opined as I watched the woman catch up to the man.

"I'm glad my lover's not that unreasonable," I retorted and smiled up at Ray, "I'm not one for chasing after a man who's actin' more like a toddler in need of a nap than my other half."

Ray dipped his head and gave me a kiss that made my toes tingle. "Different strokes for different folks, Jo. But I agree, we have enough drama without makin' mountains outta molehills all the time."

He plucked a sprig from the violet wood sorrel that was potted in a barrel planter on the wide back deck of the bed and breakfast and held it out for me.

I was shocked he'd been able to break the tiny purple flower from its vine. I took it and placed it behind my right ear as I stared at him. "How'd you do that?"

He laughed and touched my ear, moving closer to smell the flower. Whispering low, Ray made me blush from head to toe. "I've learned how to use my hands better, sweetheart. I aim to show you just how much better this evenin' after the wedding."

Ray hadn't allowed me to come visit him on his side of the veil in months, but the mention of being with him again set my heart to racing. "But you said I can't cross over again," I reminded him, keeping my voice low and sultry hoping that my enthusiasm for the idea showed in the way I moved closer to him.

His hand went around my waist and rested on my hip, the weight of it surprising me as much as his actions with the wood sorrel flower. "You ain't crossin' over darling, I am."

Sighing as we walked across the deck and out of the shadows, I happily accepted this arrangement. If it was all I could have, I'd have to be grateful for it.

Genie came out onto the deck as we gained the open French doors that Billy Jack had installed to replace an old sliding glass door two weeks before. The Drunken Rooster Bed, Breakfast, and Brewery, the name they'd settled on at last for their new business venture, would officially open the coming weekend since all the cosmetic changes had been completed.

Granny's wedding was the perfect event to do a soft open before the paying customers came pouring in for the big bluegrass festival that was coming up in a few months. Uncle Joe and his band would be performing and hosting the festival in Devil's Elbow.

I took Genie's hand as she greeted us and complimented her dress. Granny had wanted all of us to dress in varying hues of purple and Genie's dress was a divine shade of lavender that accented her summer tan. The top of the dress was a halter style design with rhinestones sprinkled across in a swirling pattern. The skirt was layers of lavender tulle, its length not too short or too long as it rested an inch above the knee.

"I think you got the best dress of all, girlfriend," I said and kissed her cheek. Ray moved in and placed an arm around her shoulders.

"I wouldn't dare say whose dress is best, but you're both pretty as a picture." My sweet beau grinned ear to ear, pleased with his diplomatic skills.

I looked down at my own dreamy outfit, a deep plum-colored maxi dress with rhinestones sprinkled across the flowy, diaphanous skirt. Granny Mack had wanted each of us to choose the style and shade of purple we loved best instead of wearing bridesmaids dresses that looked all the same. "Wait until you see Aunt Dixie," I warned him, "she puts us both to shame."

Nodding enthusiastically, Genie agreed. Right on cue, my aunt came out onto the deck, her hair piled high with rhinestone pins situated strategically to make the most of the 'do PJ had arranged. She clapped her hands sharply when she saw us and Genie and I lined up for inspection.

Ray whistled low as Aunt Dixie approached. "You ain't supposed to outshine the bride, Aunt Dixie! I think I'm gonna be busier than a bee keepin' all your admirers in line this evening."

She blushed a deep shade of pink and laughed at Ray as she looked down at her dress. "Hush now, son. This old thing has been in my closet forever."

The mauve wrap dress hugged her ample curves and I had to admit the simple lines were the perfect cut to show off her young-at-heart beauty. Several elves of the Seelie Court that had come to serve as Mr. B's groomsmen stood in a cluster not far from us, their glances showing my aunt wouldn't spend the evening without dance partners.

Before I could fix my mouth to compliment my aunt, the young lady who had pushed past me and Ray earlier, chasing after the angry gentleman, came dashing up the deck steps. She had a delicate lace handkerchief in hand and I saw her dab at her eyes as she passed us again, trying to catch her tears so they didn't ruin her makeup.

Genie sighed and went after the woman and Aunt Dixie crossed her arms and huffed. "I don't think their magic act is worth all the trouble of dealing with them two."

"So that's who they are! This evening's entertainment! What kind of trouble have they been givin' Genie?" I trained an eye on the man, who sat on the edge of the stage, a beer bottle in hand.

Aunt Dixie sighed and followed my gaze. "He's the real problem. That poor girl, his assistant, has been chasin' him around all day tryin' to talk sense to him. Nothing's good enough for him, not his room, not the food, not even the beer, though he's been swiggin' that since noon.

And he's been arguing with Billy Jack and his own dang manager over compensation. They've got free board and food and my son's paid him a handsome sum up front cause Granny just loves watchin' mortal magicians. But nothing's good enough for him. I'd have sent him packin' four hours ago if we coulda found someone else on such short notice."

It was such a shame to have drama on Granny's big day. "Would it be wrong to cast a harmony spell over the proceedings? I mean, it wouldn't harm anyone and smoothing over this drama between them would make Granny happier."

"I already tried, believe me. It's perfectly acceptable to cast spells of love, harmony and good wishes at a wedding but those two have remained unaffected. Some mortals have a strong resistance to goodwill and that one," Aunt Dixie shook her head as she eyed the magician, "has some kind of darkness in his soul."

Ray moved to stand between us. "I don't know what I can do, but if y'all can use my presence to dampen his anger I'm up for it."

"You'd have to inhabit his body to make a difference, Ray, and we're not doin' none of that. If it comes to it, Billy Jack will ask him to leave and we'll have to come up with another form of entertainment." Aunt Dixie didn't hesitate to quell Ray's concerns.

I smiled as I looked at Uncle Joe up on stage with his bluegrass band. "Let me have a word with my uncle. I bet he can settle things down a bit. No offense to you Aunt Dixie, but he has a way of makin' the men around him straighten up and fly right."

"You go right on ahead, sugar. Lord knows it can't hurt at this point." Aunt Dixie gave her blessing and I knew she'd really had more than enough of the ornery, drunken magician.

Leaving my aunt and Ray on the deck, I skipped down the steps, past the group of handsome groomsmen elves, and strode purposefully across the grass to the stage.

Before I could make my way up the steps, the magician who'd kept his pretty lady assistant in tears for the better part of the day, hopped up and blocked my way.

I crossed my arms and held my breath as his beer breath pushed out in an annoying attempt at a compliment, and wafted past my nose in a noxious cloud. Thinking of honeysuckles, I neutralized the odor.

He was speaking again, his brows drawing together in irritation. "You think you're too good to speak to me? You ain't all that pretty anyway."

Moving to step around him, I froze as his hand shot out to catch my arm. I looked down at the contact and pulled free from his grasp. Keeping my tone of voice even, I glared at him. "You ain't got a lick of sense, mister. Sit back down before you get more than your feelin's hurt."

Uncle Joe's big hand landed on the man's shoulder and the rest of the Shifty River boys surrounded us. "My mother would so enjoy the pleasure of watchin' your magic show, sir. Since this is her day, I'll spare your sorry hide for now. If you dare lay hands on any of the womenfolk gathered here, I'm gonna stomp a hole in you."

The magician cowered as the band tightened the circle around him and he stammered an apology to me. Uncle Joe gave a slight nod of his head and his boys escorted Mr. Magician back to his seat at the edge of the stage.

"I'll be glad when this whole thing is a done deal," Uncle Joe declared, wiping sweat from his brow. The evening was humid and his starched white shirt, purple vest, and untied cravat gave him little comfort.

I quickly buttoned the buttons at his throat and expertly tied his cravat. Breathing out a little breath that chilled him like a winter breeze to aid in his comfort, I smiled and admired my work. "You better look out for Missus Elsie Rose tonight. She's been circling this stage since Ray and I walked up."

At the mention of Freddie's ghost mama, Uncle Joe rolled his eyes and stretched his neck, still uncomfortable with his *get-up* as he called it. "She better look out for your friend Bonita is all I have to say about that."

His evil grin at my shocked expression was too much to ignore.

"You mean to tell me you and Bonita got somethin' goin' on? Well, I never!" I turned and looked all around for my bestie, wondering what she had been up to with my uncle.

"You have too and you plan on doin' it again tonight if my intuition is workin'." Uncle Joe's eyes sparkled with merriment as he teased me.

"That's where you're wrong. I haven't been on Ray's side of the veil since the Kudzu 500 and all that trouble the Hunts. Anyway, I came over here to get you to yank a knot in that magician fellow and you've done your part." I turned to leave and he caught my elbow.

"Don't you go messin' with Bonita. We're both old enough to do as we please, short stack."

I smiled so sweetly that butter wouldn't melt in my mouth. Keeping my cool, I pretended I wouldn't make a beeline to Bonita's side and grill her right quick before the wedding ceremony started. "You better get back on that stage and get your fiddle fingers ready to play the weddin' march, mister."

He gave me a long look and pointed two fingers from his eyes to mine to indicate he was watching me. Kissing his cheek, I laughed as his whiskers tickled my lips and left him hoping that I didn't skip on over to where Bonita stood with PJ beside the groomsmen, and find out what they'd been up to.

2

There wasn't a dry eye to be found as Granny came out onto the deck, a vision in her wedding dress that was tea-length and a glorious shade of aubergine that made her silver hair sparkle even without the aid of the rhinestone combs the rest of us had employed.

Since Uncle Joe was supplying the musical portion of the ceremony, Billy Jack was the one to walk her down the aisle, across the grass now kissed with evening dew, to hand her to Mr. B before taking his place in the line of groomsmen that stretched out into the soft darkness of the night. Freddie stood beside Mr. B as his best man, his tux matching all those of the Seelie court elves gathered around, and I gave a little wave of my fingers as our eyes met past his uncle and my grandmother.

He was looking mighty fine and I thought it must

be because of the love he'd found with Sally Hunt. They'd spent a lot of time together. Freddie had kept The Value Vintage open for me while I'd been camping up in the hills for a good long while before Granny's wedding and she'd been his constant companion.

After the fight with the Covey brothers, and the appearance of the soul streak in my hair, Granny had gently nudged me to go off into the woods alone and work on mastering my summoning stone. Since I knew Uncle Joe and Aunt Dixie wouldn't stop nudging me in that direction either, I'd took off two weeks before the wedding even though I wanted to help Granny plan the ceremony.

Now as I watched my family unite with Freddie's, I was happy I'd taken Granny's advice. Those weeks in the woods had been difficult, but the summoning stone was now under my complete control. Ray and I had tested it when I came back, just to be certain I hadn't been fooled by the enigmatic nature of the stone. He'd stayed behind in Devil's Elbow with Delilah during my absence so we were more than happy to see each other again. That first night back, I'd left the stone on my bedside table to see whether it would suck me into the other side with Ray like it had done in the past. As much as we wanted to see one another, I'd stayed on my side night after night.

Though the stone's surface still swirled impatiently whenever I held it and I felt the pull it tried to exert on me, I was its master now.

Thanks to an ancient book Granny had given me before I left, I knew the rituals I had to practice to tame the stone by reading it carefully the first few nights alone in the woods. There was a heap of purifying on my part and resisting on the part of the stone.

At one point, on the night before I finally broke through and learned how to harness its power, I thought I would be lost to the stone's desires to control me. My ancestors came and danced around me, their shadows flickering in the light of my campfire, their voices raised in a dialect foreign to my ears, though I knew every word they chanted.

I shivered as the goosebumps from that memory formed on my bare arms. Granny and Mr. B were kissing and everyone had begun clapping and whistling as Uncle Joe struck up the band in a bluegrass sort of jig.

Granny and her new husband turned and walked back down the aisle together and hurried to the spot behind the stage where Billy Jack and Genie had set up a dance floor under a large canopy strung with more lights. Uncle Joe and the Shifty River Band moved their equipment around as we all gathered on the dance floor so they could see us as they played the first song the bride and groom would dance to and kick off a long night of celebration.

Ray took my hand and I walked into the shadows with him, the straps of my satin purple pumps dangling from one finger since I'd shucked them as soon as possible after the wedding ceremony.

I laughed as his ghostly breath tickled my ear. He was as frisky as a new colt and I couldn't rightly blame him. Spending time apart had the effect of causing him to change his mind about advising me to rethink our relationship. I whispered as he kissed my ear. "We need to be out there for the first dance, Ray."

"And we will be, Jo. I just wanted you to myself for a minute. Seeing you standin' up there with the other bridesmaids made me think of us having our weddin' someday soon. I know it won't be the same as it should have been, but if you're sure you want me for the rest of your natural, and unnatural life, then we should do it."

I was shocked by his proposal of sorts, but thrilled by it too. "Oh honey, do you really mean it? Don't pull my leg when it comes to a weddin' Ray Dang Davis! You know I'd marry you in a hot second."

Leaning into him, I laid my head against his chest,

surprised by the faint heartbeat I heard. Maybe it was the racing of my own in my ears at the excitement of having my boyfriend ask me to marry him for a second time when it was much harder for us to be together.

The strains of a twangy, country slow dance ballad drifted to us and we reluctantly left the shelter of the shadows. Granny and Mr. B slow danced across the dance floor as all our friends and family circled around them taking pictures and singing the sweet words of the song in a happy chorus of voices.

Once the second stanza began, couples joined them from the circle and I stood by Ray swaying to the music, still singing along softly.

"We'll dance together at our own weddin', I promise," he whispered as his arm went around my shoulders. As I turned to smile at him, the magician who'd bugged me earlier bumped into me as he staggered around.

"A purty gal like you oughta be out there dancin'!" His words slurred as he grabbed my arm and pulled me out into the crowd of dancing couples. Since it was Granny's wedding, I didn't want to cause a fuss but I wasn't dancing with his drunken backside for nothing.

Instead of yelling or getting physical with him, I looked down at his beefy hand on my arm and whispered a spell that loosened his grip and sent him stumbling away from me. I tried to send another spell after him, one to sober him up a bit and put some sense back in his head, but he turned tail and took off across the dance floor like a ghost was after him.

When I saw Ray streak past me, I laughed. A ghost *was* after the poor, silly magician but I didn't think he could really see Ray. Leaving the dance floor, I wandered to the tables set up for a wedding supper and smiled when I spotted Bonita sitting all alone. "Mind if I join you? Since you can't dance with Uncle Joe right now and I can't dance with Ray, we might as well keep each other company."

Bonita shook her head, making her shiny curls that were up in a lovely cascading 'do bounce with enthusiasm. "Now how you gonna come over here and accuse me of watchin' Joe Mack on that stage over there?"

The twinkle of merriment in her chocolate brown eyes delighted me. She knew dang well she'd been watching my uncle. "That dog won't hunt, sweet friend. Y'all been tradin' looks back and forth since I got here, at least. But I can't think of a sweeter woman for him. Just in case you were wonderin' what I thought."

My bestie snorted and sipped from her fruity drink in its blue-colored mason jar. I thought I might need one of those before long. The night was perfect but a little humid and my tastebuds were parched. A mosquito whined by my ear and I quickly sent him, and any of his friends, off to some other part of the woods with a lantana, aka verbena, spell. My specially crafted repellant was better than anything you could buy in the big box stores.

Bonita batted her eyelashes at me and sipped her drink again. "I saw you and Ray over there in the shadows. Seems like y'all are closer than ever. It was almost like I could see your soul twined with his. What's that all about?"

I admired the pivot from her love life to mine, but I wasn't letting her off that easy. Pointing at the soul streak in my hair, I only sighed. "Long story and I don't know quite how to give you the short of it cause there's just too much to tell. But he did just propose to me again!"

My grin bloomed from the depths of my heart just talking about my man and I could see Bonita was genuinely happy for me, but there was a crease of worry in her normally unlined forehead. "Well sugar, you know I'm as happy as a lark for the two of you but only if you're absolutely certain that's what you want for the rest of your life."

I was more sure now than I'd been the first time I'd accepted a marriage proposal from Ray. "Nothing would make me happier, Bonita. Cross my heart. I can't see my life without him by my side."

We sat in comfortable silence after that watching all the dancers. After three more songs had passed, Zeke and Floyd, Billy Jack's mechanic friends, rang the bell over by the barbecue pit and hollered out that supper was served.

Me and Bonita hopped up and joined the line forming around the buffet tables that groaned with so much good food. There were baked beans that smelled of bacon and rum and carmelized brown sugar, and whipped cream corn salad sitting pretty beside Granny's heavenly succotash. Bowls of chow chow sat here and there while pickled slaw drew my eye with its bright colors. Corn fritters rested in little red, plastic baskets with fresh, creamy honey butter on the side. My eyes were bigger than my stomach, though. I filled up one plate with just sides before I even got to the meat Zeke and Fred had been cooking all day.

Freddie and Sally appeared at my side with two plates of gloriously prepared barbecue beef, pork, and chicken. "If you fill up another plate of sides, we'll share all our goodies with you, Jolene."

I smiled at the happy couple, hoping they'd be the next to tie the knot. "That sounds like a plan, y'all.

Since the line is looping around and going back down, I can fill up another plate lickety split!."

In two shakes of a lamb's tail, I was seated at a table with Granny, Mr. B., Freddie and Sally, Aunt Dixie and some elf friend she'd charmed to her side, and Billy Jack and Genie. Sitting with my entire family made me happier than a pig in mud and I got down to the business of eating.

By the time I was half way through my meal, I noticed Uncle Joe wasn't sitting with us. As I expected, he was with Bonita at a table where PJ was flirting with yet another elf of the Seelie court. I wondered how long the handsome elves would stay in Devil's Elbow after the wedding.

Another fellow caught my eye and it wasn't because he was handsome. The frisky magician was rambling around from table to table embarrassing himself with the ladies and upsetting husbands and boyfriends left and right. Most sent him on his way without raising a ruckus, but when I saw him leaning on Nadean Bodean, I held my breath. Walker was a huge teddy bear of a man, but he didn't cotton to anyone putting their hands on his missus.

Uncle Joe, Billy Jack, and I hopped up in unison and made a beeline to the Bodean's table. Trouble was, Walker was already on his feet and had the man lifted off the ground with one hand. Several other men gathered and egged on the bait and tackle shop owner with chants of *fight, fight, fight* as we tried to intervene.

Before my kinfolk could get control of the situation, Walker planted his fist in the magician's face with force that would leave a mark before the clock struck midnight, which was only about an hour away.

The magician's assistant came quickly, but her steps were cautious. She pulled on the man's arm as Walker released him. Thankfully, she led him up onto the deck away from the supper tables.

I followed after them with Billy Jack while Uncle Joe sorted Walker and Nadean. I heard the Shifty River Boys break into a popular number to distract the guests. Hoping their quick thinking would soothe everyone's ruffled feathers, I stood beside my cousin on the deck as he gave the magician what-for.

"Now, I ain't gonna throw you out tonight, but you can't come back out here and sabotage my Granny's celebration," Billy Jack said and looked from the magician to his assistant, "but since you've been paid for a show, I expect somebody's gonna give us a show."

The assistant gave a small, tight smile and held out her hand. "I'm Jessi, pleased to meet you. I can do it in a pinch if you don't mind me bein' nervous and all. Let me get him upstairs and settled in for the night and I'll come back down and run through the routine. I know it by heart, after all. I may need someone I can saw in half, though."

Billy Jack shook the woman's free hand and grinned wide as the Mississippi. "We don't mind at all, miss. And my cousin, Jolene, why she'd love to be sawed in half!"

3

I elbowed my cousin and shook my head as Jessi led the magician inside the bed and breakfast. "Oh no you don't! You're the one who hired that handsy heathen, not me. You can be sawed in half and see how you like it."

"Aww Jolene! Don't be like that. She ain't really gonna saw you in half, it's just an illusion. Besides, you want to see Granny happy don't you? I seen that box they use and ain't no way I can fit inside it." He held up a hand and measured from the top of my head to just below his chin to illustrate our height difference.

Dang it if he didn't have a valid point. He was big as a danged ox and twice as obstinate. Sighing with irritation, I stomped my foot for extra emphasis. "Oh alright! But I'm only doing this for Granny."

Billy Jack slapped his leg and hooted in victory. I

shot him a mean side-eye and tried to hold onto the fact that I was doing it for Granny. Ray appeared at my side, his voice soothing. "You'll be perfect for the part, Jo! Now how many folks in these parts can say they got cut in half and lived to tell the tale?"

As much as I hated to admit it, he had a point. Our friends and neighbors would get a kick out of having someone they knew sawed in half up on that stage. I knew I'd spend the next few months being teased about it everywhere I went in Devil's Elbow.

"I guess it ain't no worse than having folks think I'm off in the head for talkin' to somebody who ain't there." I smiled up at my boyfriend with forced enthusiasm and he kissed the tip of my nose.

Billy Jack ignored us and looked back at the French doors as we all left the deck. "I just wish that magician feller had been less lecherous and more professional. Way he was goin', aggravating all the ladies, it's a wonder Walker was the only man to jerk a knot in him."

I shrugged, eager to get back to my meal. "You know hillbilly women. If he'd been more than a nuisance, one of us would have snatched him up before any of the men could have been bothered. He just happened to run up on the wrong one with Walker."

By the time I'd made it back to my plate, questions about the magic show were flying all around the table. "Jolene," Granny asked, her expression reminding me of Old Blue when he was frettin' over whether he might get a soup bone, "is that feller gonna come back and carry on with the show or what?"

Licking barbecue sauce off my fingers, I smiled at her trying to reassure my sweet grandmother that she wouldn't miss her magic show. "He's down for the count, I'm afraid. But that assistant of his says she can manage and your grandson volunteered me to get sawed in half tonight."

The table erupted in oohs, ahhs, and some laughter. I felt like giving them all the side eye but Ray smiled at me and I recalled that my participation would keep Granny happy.

"You're so brave, Jo!" Genie said and blew me a kiss. Aunt Dixie shook her head and looked at her son. "You better hope that magician's assistant knows how to work that saw, son. Jolene comes in handy when it comes to keepin' you outta trouble."

Mr. B cleared his throat and we all glanced at him, giving him the respect as his position alongside Granny as the head of the family. "Our Jolene is in no danger, even if the young lady isn't as skilled as her partner. I'll personally see to it that no harm comes to her and that the show is a wondrous one for my sweet bride."

He kissed Granny's hand and a hush fell over the table. "Why Elven," Granny sighed, her eyelashes batting coquettishly, "I think you're more romantic now than when you were a young elf."

Seeing them so in love melted the rest of my resolve and as soon as I spied Jessi waving at me from the deck, I rose from my spot at the table. "Here goes nothin' y'all!"

The whoops and hollering that followed me as I picked my way through the supper tables made my cheeks flame red with the heat of embarrassment.

For her part, Jessi looked adorable in the top hat and tails she'd donned. The ill fit showed they were clearly made for the magician, but she certainly looked the part she was about to play. Her warm smile put me at ease and I followed her as we went up on stage. Uncle Joe and his band had cleared off their instruments and apparently hauled up the infamous box I'd climb into before the show was over. I eyed it curiously, wondering just how the illusion worked. I had an idea it involved a pair of fake legs, or so I hoped.

Jessi's lead was easy to follow as we went through the simple routine of the show and more than once I was tempted to work little spells to help her through some of the nerves she showed from being the center of attention. Overall, she did a bang up job of covering for her inebriated, offensive partner.

When it came time to saw me in half, she moved the long box that looked too much like a coffin centerstage. Despite the fact that I knew she wasn't really going to cut me, I regretted stuffing myself full of barbecue. My stomach gurgled and I swallowed hard to push away my own fit of nerves.

Jessi took my hand and led me behind the box and lifted the hinged lid for me to climb inside. At once, I saw the gist of the trick. Hiding my surprise at the revelation as best I could, I climbed into my half of the box and waited while another girl, already secured inside the second box, took off my purple heels and put them on her feet and pushed them through her end of the box. I laid down and rested my neck on the cushion that lined my end where there was an opening for my head.

Jessi built the tension by sashaying around on stage with the saw in hand. She asked Billy Jack to bring some wood from the woodpile over by the barbecue pit. When he lumbered up on stage with his arms loaded with logs he'd sawed up for the barbecue, I prayed Jessi wouldn't turn the saw over to him. He'd love nothing more than to saw me in half.

The next thing I knew, Jessi did hand him the saw,

but only so he could saw the logs he'd brought up to show the audience. I supposed she was trying to show the crowd that the saw blade was the real deal.

After my cousin finished his part in the show, Jessi sent him back to his seat. She came around the box holding the saw up over her head. When she had the audience on the edge of their seats, she made a production out of slowly sawing back and forth, wincing as she went. I made silly faces and cried out in agony as I cast a little spell for gory sound effects that rattled poor Jessi so that she released the saw and jumped back, a squeal escaping her lips.

The audience rippled with nervous laughter and I hollered for her to take the saw out. The poor woman was terrified as she grabbed the saw and pulled it away. She stared at the shiny, clean saw blade, her eyes round as two quarters.

"Go on ahead and pull her apart gal!" Someone yelled from the audience.

Jessi found her wits and unlatched the hinges that held the two halves of the box together. When she rolled the two pieces apart, the girl in the other box wiggled her feet and I hollered out as loud as I could. "I always thought my better half would be a handsome feller!"

This drew laughter and groans from the crowd and Jessi hurried to put the box back together. She placed the saw under the box and moved to the front of the stage. "Now listen up, everybody. We have to count to three together and say the magic words to put Miss Jolene back together again."

Uncle Joe hollered out from his seat by Bonita. "Well, what's the magic word?"

"Abracadabra!" Jessi said and giggled.

The crowd counted to three at her signal and then shouted the magic word.

I threw open the box's lid and climbed out, remembering to grab my heels from my other half and slide my feet back in them before standing and walking out in front of the box. Taking a bow, I hugged my middle and moaned. Poor Jessi gave me her apologies but Instead of torturing her further, I rubbed my tummy and clapped for her, encouraging the crowd to join in.

I winked as I took her hand and held it up in triumph. Shrugging, Jessi bowed with me as the audience continued to clap, whoop, holler, and whistle.

Leaving my new friend with a little guilt at having had fun at her expense, I hurried to the family table as the rounds of wedding toasts began. Uncle Joe and his band went up on stage to help Jessi and I sent my waiter, who'd just given me a flute of spritzy apple cider, to her side to deliver her a well-earned flute with my apologies for putting her on while I was in the box.

Jessi lifted it to me in salute and I returned the gesture. Something told me we could have been good friends if she ever spent much time in Devil's Elbow.

By the time another hour had passed and all the toasts and congratulations were finished, Granny and Mr. B led us all back to the dance floor for another slow dance before they left on their honeymoon.

We showered them in birdseed that Granny insisted we use since it wouldn't harm the birds that nested all around the bed and breakfast. Most of the Seelie Court elves went with my grandmother and her new husband in an impressive motorcade that would see them to the airport in Knoxville for their red-eye flight on a private jet owned by the elves. A secret island, that was also Seelie property, would be their honeymoon destination. Granny had shown me pictures of the beach and the luxurious hut that sat out over the water and I knew I wanted to go there with Ray one day.

Turning to my sweet, spirited beau, I gave him the look that meant I was more than ready to sneak off to our room at the bed and breakfast. "Now that Granny's gone, I'm ready to call it a night. I'm glad we decided to stay here instead of heading home so late."

Ray agreed as he kissed my forehead and took my hand. "I believe Billy Jack said most of the folks here are staying the night, even those without a room. He's lettin' them camp out in the field out there past the dance floor."

My cousin was getting smarter about running a business and in short order. As Ray and I climbed the steps to the deck, I gazed around at all the work Billy Jack and Genie had done on this old place. When we were all kids, we used to come out here every summer when it was Camp Athiamiowee. The land the bed and breakfast sat on had an old game trail that ran through it and that was the Shawnee name for the trail. The word meant *Warriors Trail*.

Ray was obviously feeling as proud as I was. "They done good, the two of 'em. I reckon when it's time for their weddin', I might actually be okay with walkin' Genie down the aisle to hand her over to Billy Jack. I sure as shootin' never thought I'd say that."

He chuckled and I felt a warmth fill my chest. Ray and Billy Jack had come a good long way as far as tolerating each other. "Come on, you old softie. Let's practice our own honeymoon." I pushed open the French doors and led him inside.

My eyes flew open and I sat up, my body trembling in fear. I sat stock still listening, my ears straining for some sound, wondering why such dread filled me from head to toe. As my eyes adjusted to the dim light filtering through the curtains of our room, I remembered where we were.

I must have had a nightmare that woke me in a state of fight or flight. Focusing on breathing slowly, I looked around the room for Ray. He wasn't beside me in the bed and a little bit of fear jumped back up in my chest.

"Ray!" I whispered stridently, swinging my feet out of the bed.

Shoot! He didn't answer which meant he'd more than likely left the room. I crept over to the bedroom door and placed a hand on the doorknob. As I turned it, a scream tore through the bed and breakfast that nearly gave me a heart attack. I don't know what possessed me to take off like a shot out of the relative safety of our room, but I was out and down the main stairs in record time.

Drawing up short on the last step, I stared at Jessi standing over a crumpled body with a knife in her hand. Genie had just come in when I did and we looked at each other in utter disbelief.

"This ain't what it looks like y'all," Jessi whispered, her eyes pleading with us to believe her.

"Is he dead?" I blurted out, moving slowly toward Jessi and the figure splayed out on the floor right in front of the check-in desk.

Billy Jack came in from the front porch, cell phone in hand. "Deader than a doornail, that's for sure. He ain't moved since we found Jessi here standin' over him."

Ray came up behind me, his hand resting on my shoulder. "Don't go near him, Jolene. It's the magician. Billy Jack's called the law. No need in messin' up the crime scene more than Jessi already has."

Genie moved closer to the magician's assistant. "What happened, Jessi? We all know he was drunker than Cooter Brown tonight. If he was tryin' to hurt you, I reckon the law will take that into consideration."

Jessi dropped the knife and stared at her hands. They shook uncontrollably as she looked around for something to wipe off the magician's blood. Her voice trembled as she looked at Genie and then me. "I didn't kill him, I loved him!"

4

Genie brought in a tray stacked with coffee cups and sat it on the big coffee table in the bed and breakfast's sprawling living room. Billy Jack followed with a silver urn full of hot coffee.

When the Cumberland Gap police arrived, we'd all been herded into the living room and no one was to leave the premises until their one detective had spoken with everyone present, including all the guests who'd stayed over, even the ones still sleeping in the tents out back.

"It's gonna be a long day," Genie sighed, her eyes going to the plate glass window that looked out over the wide front lawn that was now filled with police cars and an ambulance that hadn't needed it's siren on its way out to the bed and breakfast.

Billy Jack kneaded her shoulders and kissed the

top of her head. "It sure ain't how I imagined the openin' of our business going, but there's nothing for it but to let the police do their job. I heard the one deputy out on the deck sayin' they're callin' in the state police to help since they're such a small outfit."

I poured cups of coffee for us all and tried to cheer up my cousin and his fiancee. "This wasn't the real grand opening though. By the time next weekend rolls around, it'll be like this never happened."

A familiar voice interrupted my pep talk and I groaned in disbelief as I turned to find Sheriff Quinn lounging by the living room door. "Oh, I don't think anyone's gonna wanna stay here when the word gets out that a murder done took place. With your family's track record, it's no wonder a crime has already been committed here."

Billy Jack's voice thundered his irritation as he left Genie's side determined to get his hands on the sheriff. I moved quick as lightning to get between them. "Now, hold on cousin. You can't go messin' with him even though he's eggin' you on."

"He ain't even got jurisdiction out here, and he sure ain't with the state police." Billy Jack strained against my arm as I tried to block him from getting to Sheriff Quinn.

"He's the law, though, and the sooner everything is sorted out, the better it is for you and Genie." I tried to reason with Billy Jack but it wasn't because I cared for Sheriff Quinn.

Thankfully, my cousin stepped back once my words sank in.

The sheriff couldn't leave well enough alone and chose to poke the bear. "You think you can fool everybody with this here fancy new business, but I've got my eye on you son. One of these days, you're gonna slip up and I'm gonna be there."

The sheriff from Cumberland Gap came in and clapped Sheriff Quinn on the back before Billy Jack could make another go at the man. "Good to see you Delbert! It's been too long. Mama said just the other day I ought to call you over for Sunday dinner."

"Cousin, I reckon it's been an age since I saw my kinfolks just over the ridge! I'll stop by and see Auntie Pearl on my way back to Devil's Elbow. Now, I hate to tell you, but this bunch here done caused all kinds of trouble for me. I expect they'll keep you busy now." Sheriff Quinn turned to us and nodded, his grin showing how happy he was for us to see that the Cumberland Gap sheriff was his kin.

Instead of arguing with the sheriff over what kind of trouble we did or did not cause him, I moved to the coffee table and sat to pour coffee for people who were drifting in from the back deck. Jessi came in behind a group of Billy Jack's friends and I was surprised the police hadn't stuffed her into the back of one of their cruisers just yet. My heart went out to her. She looked lost and confused, and her face was tear stained, her eyes rimmed red. Taking a cup of the hot coffee to her on a saucer with sugar cubes and a tiny pod of creamer, I rubbed her back as she gave me a trembling smile. "Hey now, it's gonna be okay. They'll find out who did it and see that justice is served."

The poor girl looked like her heart was about to break plumb in two and I took back the cup of coffee as she pushed it into my hand and fell apart in my arms. Sheriff Quinn came over and I gave him an evil eye for the ages. "She ain't up for talkin' to anybody right about now. Let her cry her eyes out in peace, won't you?"

To my surprise, the sheriff moved off without a bit of trouble, but I could see he would be on her like a duck on a june bug the minute her tears dried up. It was good to think he had a bit of decency to him, though.

"Thank, you," Jessi whispered against my shoulder, hiccups punctuating her words.

"You'd have done the same for me, I reckon. I'm awful sorry you lost someone so dear to you. I thought maybe the two of you were romantically entangled, but now I can see it must have been serious. A woman doesn't cry like this over a man unless he's been something special to her."

Unfortunately, I knew that kind of heartache all too well. I'd spent a good five days mourning Ray from the moment I learned he died until the morning after his funeral when his ghost had come to me in my room at Granny's house. I wouldn't wish that pain on a single soul, friend or foe.

Jessi finally let go and pulled herself together as best she could. "I didn't think anybody noticed, honestly. I mean, Roger wasn't exactly lovey-dovey lately. We even argued tonight."

So the magician's name was Roger. I looked her in the eye and spoke quietly. I didn't want the chance to miss out on a confession or information that might crack the case if she really hadn't run him through with a butcher knife.

"After you sent him off to bed and we did the show together?" I really wasn't trying to usurp the police by asking, but I was too nosy for my own good.

"He woke up and came to my room hoping to make up for being a jerk but I told him he needed to think about his drinkin'. It had gone too far. Rewarding him after a night of bad behavior didn't seem like the right thing to do. Now, I guess I should have given in like always and maybe he'd still be alive." Her lower lip trembled again but I refused to let her think such thoughts.

"Hey now, it's not your fault he's...gone. You weren't the only one he was spatting with last night, remember? I can't believe any of my friends or neighbors would have hurt him, though. He was obnoxious for sure, but that usually only gets you a whoopin' you won't soon forget up here in the mountains." I tapped a finger on my bottom lip trying to think of who might have been out for blood at the bed and breakfast.

Jessi glanced over at Sheriff Quinn and then took hold of my hand. "Listen, before they take me away for murder, I need you to know I didn't do it. You've been so kind to me and I don't have any friends nearby. When I followed him downstairs after he knocked on my door this morning, we argued on the deck. Arty came out then, and I left them out there and went back to bed."

Surprised by the fact that she felt some kinship to me, enough to confide in me some things she hadn't even shared with the police yet, I tried to reassure her. "Surely they can't think you were the killer just because you found him. And who the heck is Arty anyway? I haven't seen anyone else around here that I don't know." Glancing around the room, I searched for a face in the crowd that was unfamiliar to me.

Sheriff Quinn was crossing the room headed for me and Jessi and she squeezed my hand hard. "Arty is our business manager. He'd been arguing with Roger for weeks but neither one would tell me what was going on and I didn't pry. I was just happy to see my check still comin' each month. Now I wish I'd stayed around and eavesdropped on them this morning."

Before I could formulate a plan to try and help Jessi, the sheriff came and led her away. It didn't feel right watching her go with him and I knew deep down she wasn't a killer.

Ray appeared at my side, his arm going around my waist. "You don't know her from Adam's housecat, Jo. It might have been a crime of passion. She did have the dang knife in her hand when we found her."

"I know it looks bad, but something tells me she wasn't the killer." I looked up at Ray hoping he'd trust my intuition.

"Something besides her own word? I sure hope you got more than that to go on." My boyfriend shook his head in doubt.

Billy Jack and Genie joined us and I worried for the both of them. This wasn't their grand opening, but that was coming soon. Next weekend to be exact. Having a grisly murder at their check-in desk wasn't exactly the kind of publicity they would have wanted.

"You reckon there's any way we can keep the news

of the murder out of the spotlight until after the grand opening?" Genie asked, her mind and mine obviously on the same wavelength.

My cousin crossed his arms and scowled as the sheriff of Cumberland Gap announced to the room that everyone was free to go but not so far that he couldn't reach them if needs be. "As fast as word travels in these hills and hollers? That's a big no, sweetheart. The best we can do is make sure everything is perfect when our guests for next weekend begin to arrive. We've got five days to figure it out. I'm thinkin' we might just keep Uncle Joe and his Shifty River Boys on retainer so's we have some good music on hand. And Mama'll bake us up some good stuff for the breakfast buffet, too."

Ray tried to join in and do what he could. "I'll be happy to add to the lore of the place and haunt it a bit if you want."

Genie and I both looked at him like he'd lost his mind. She tried to be diplomatic as she refused him. "Maybe another time, big brother. I think it might be too soon with the magician's murder and all."

Leaving my family in the front room to figure out the best plan of action, I followed the stragglers from the night before as they filtered out the front door behind the police. The check-in desk was still closed off with police tape, but I tiptoed behind the counter anyway and whispered a little spell to help me see into the dark corners and places the police might have missed.

Nothing out of the ordinary appeared as I knelt down and tried to concentrate on who might have been with Roger the magician right before he was murdered while my hands searched the floor behind the desk.

My fingers grazed the floorboards searching for any trace of a clue but my mind only drew a blank. I couldn't use the sight to see Roger or his murderer without something that belonged to either one of them.

Just as I was about to give up and rejoin my kin in the front room, I felt something small roll beneath my fingers and froze. The image of the magician's face flickered before my eyes and I looked down to see the knife that had killed him in my own hand, buried to the hilt in his chest. My hand was covered in a black, leather glove so I couldn't tell if I was supposed to be male or female.

Falling back on my rear end behind the check-in desk, I panted for breath. I'd seen the man's final moments on earth and the shock that filled his face was all I could think of. He'd been shocked by the identity of his killer.

I pushed myself up off the floor and realized I had

picked up something from under the desk in the midst of the awful vision. As I opened my hand, a glitter of black obsidian greeted me. It was a small cylinder of onyx with a silver snake wrapped around it, a pendant of some sort as far as I could tell. The strength of its magick sang to me as I held it, but it felt different to me than any magick I knew.

Genie called my name and I hastily stepped from behind the check-in desk and shoved the pendant into the pocket of my robe. It was time to get dressed and get busy figuring out who the killer was before an innocent woman was railroaded for murder.

$$5$$

The sight of The Value Vintage lifted a weight from my shoulders I hadn't known I was carrying around. Genie and Billy Jack insisted I go back home and see about Delilah. I knew I also needed to spell Freddie so he and Sally could do a day trip over to Dollywood they'd been wanting to take since before I went off into the woods on my camping trip.

Beside me, Ray sighed with contentment as we went inside and I knew he was happy to be home again, too. With me out in the woods, he'd been visiting his mama's house. Mrs. Davis was over the moon to have him home with her, but even as a ghost he'd learned you can't always go home again. Unlike me, she'd wanted to know where he was at all hours. I could understand her anxiety, but I didn't dare get in between them. As much as I love his mama, that was a row Ray would have to hoe on his own as far as I was concerned.

Before I could even say how do you do to Freddie or Sally, Delilah rushed to my side, her purr dialed up as far as it could go.

"Hey girl," I crooned as I bent to pick her up. She buried her head in the crook of my neck and I laughed as her whiskers tickled me. Seeing my familiar was one of the greatest joys of my life. Her presence was a comfort I cherished more than I could say. I hoped she knew just how much she meant to me.

Sally came to hug me, her smile genuine. "We've missed you so much, lady. It's been a crash course in business minding the shop for you, and Delilah's been such a sweet girl. I wish I could find a feline like her."

I laughed as my familiar licked my jawline. "She is one of a kind, but I don't mind sharing her from time to time."

Freddie came over and Delilah continued her purring as he stroked her bright, white fur. "I think she was getting antsy right before you guys came in. She's been in her spot at the front window since we opened up this morning. I was a little worried you might stay out at the bed and breakfast after word got back here about the murder."

I was hoping news hadn't traveled that fast, but I surely wasn't surprised it had. "I'm only back for a few days so you don't quit me for good," I said as I lowered my voice and glanced around the shop to be sure we were alone. "I found something out there, after the police left, that I need to investigate. There's magick at play that I don't understand. I wish Granny wasn't off on her honeymoon. I can't bother her with this."

Freddie held out his hand and I stared at it before shaking my head. "Come on, Jo. Let me see. Maybe I can help figure it out. I am an elf you know. We have a legendary collective memory. If I don't know it, no one does."

The bell above the door of the VV rang out, jarring me from my pow wow with Freddie, and two folks walked in. My elf friend dropped his hand and gave me a look that said he wasn't giving up just yet.

Sally greeted my customers and I moved behind the cash register with Delilah so I could get myself back into the mood for working with the public. Being out in the woods for weeks alone had been the best thing for me after we figured out Maybelle's murder, but I was truly happy to be home again.

Freddie followed me and kept his voice low. "If my powers don't fail me, you've got some kind of relic in your pocket and its vibe is ancient. Something tells me that whoever owns it, they ain't about to let it stay missin' for too long. Best you let me cloak the fact that you possess it unless you're hankin' for a showdown that'll make the one out in the bottom with the Covey brothers look like child's play."

Since Sally was keeping my customers busy, and failing counsel from my granny, I followed Freddie to the back room and showed him the pendant I'd found at the bed and breakfast. His sharp intake of breath startled me.

"If my great uncle were here, he'd have that thing taken to the Seelie Court immediately and turned over to the Queen. Will you let me have it, Jo? I think that's the best course of action." Freddie nearly pleaded with me as he glanced over his shoulder.

Since I was sure the relic was tied to whoever it was that murdered Roger the magician, and seemed to be the one clue I had to go on to help Jessi and protect the bed and breakfast, I shook my head. "I can't do that just yet, Freddie. After the murderer is found and my cousin's business is in the clear, I'll be more than happy to have this thing taken off my hands."

I meant it too, the pendant was giving off some sort of energy that gave me a dreadful, awful feeling.

My friend clearly disagreed with my decision, but

he knew it was pointless to argue. "In that case, I'll offer what protection I can since I know this thing could cause a whole heap of trouble. Put it on the table over there and come stand behind me. It's been a while since I last worked a spell like the one I'm about to cast."

I did as he said, but wondered what was so diffi-cult about a cloaking spell. I could do one of those with my eyes closed. Freddie picked up on my doubt. "I was wrong. A cloaking spell won't last long on an ancient relic. Instead, I'll need to weave a spell to block its energy while also casting another that will protect you and the rest of the town in case the owner is strong enough to locate it even with my formidable powers hiding it away."

I didn't try to argue his point, and his words reminded me to question Billy Jack and Aunt Dixie about the wards on the bed and breakfast. It seemed odd that someone wielding a different magick had been able to cross over their doorstep. My own wards had been broken before, so I knew such things could happen. I hastily stepped behind Freddie as he began to weave the magick he possessed as an elf.

It wasn't the same as my witchy powers. He didn't fool around whispering spells or gathering herbs and arranging them in a pattern around the pendant. He simply bowed his head and though his lips moved, he made not a sound I could hear.

But someone, or something did, and the pendant was, for lack of a better word, wrapped in a magick as strong as my own as it rose from its place on the table. Freddie's energy expanded to fill the room and I understood at once why he'd told me to get behind him. If I'd stayed by the table with the pendant, my own energy would have warred with his. By being at his back, I was spared the conflict our different forms of magick would have sparked.

My friend was wiser than me in many things, and I made a mental note of this information as I knew very little about the magick elves possessed and how it worked with other magickal beings, or in this case, how it might not work with other magickal beings.

The pendant fell unceremoniously back to the table and Freddie swore gently under his breath. My happy-go-lucky elf friend, who could charm the birds right out of the trees, never spoke like that and it worried me. I took hold of his arm as I came around to face him. "What's happened, Freddie?"

His smile was tight and I could tell the use of his magick had affected him as he brushed off my concern. "It's nothing, Jo. The spells are cast, but I can't say for sure how long they'll last. You best put that thing away and hope the killer is found quick for all our sakes."

Freddie wasn't being completely honest with me, I could tell that much from the regret in his eyes. But he'd done all he could to help me and I was grateful for that much. "I promise I'll get to the bottom of this lickety-split. I bet I'll have the whole thing solved before you and Sally get back from Dollywood."

I left him and retrieved the pendant from the table. The energy it had been putting out into the world was muted and I grinned in spite of the situation. Freddie had done me a solid watching the shop, and another one in hiding the pendant from its owner. In spite of the murder at my cousin's fledgling business, things were looking up.

"I don't think it's such a good idea for me to leave right now. Uncle Elven sure wouldn't like it if I left you and Ray here alone with this relic in your hands. We can always go to Dollywood after everything is settled with the murder." Freddie's voice hid the disappointment I could feel flowing from him.

"No, I won't have it any other way. Your uncle and my granny would have a lot to say about this pendant, I'm sure, but they aren't here. We can handle this. You've done your part and now it's my turn. Two days aren't going to be the end of the world. Besides, Sally needs time alone with you away from Devil's Elbow. Anybody can see the sadness in her spirit."

Freddie ran a hand through his raven hair. "Darn it all, Jo, I know you're right. I can't expect Sally to keep giving me her all without taking her away from here even for a little while. She loves it here, and I know she never wants to leave, but a romantic getaway would do a world of good."

Shoving the pendant back in my pocket, I pushed him back through the beaded curtain to the front of the shop. "Go and get packin' while I take care of my business. We'll see each other when y'all get back."

Thankfully, Sally was waiting for us behind the counter and Freddie led her upstairs while I turned to the man and woman who were browsing the display of postcards by the front door.

They whispered stridently back and forth and Delilah circled my ankles, her anxiety reaching me as the pair pulled out three cards from the rack before making their way to the register. Ray was nearby, and I felt safer with him downstairs with me. Reminding myself to smile, I greeted the strange pair warmly. "Hey y'all! Welcome to Devil's Elbow. Is there anything you'd like besides those postcards? I've got some glass pieces from an artisan friend over in West Virginia there in the far corner. She's done pieces for the first ladies that still sit on display in the White House."

Instead of looking impressed, the two seemed distracted as they gazed at me. The man was much younger than the lady and I wondered for a moment if they were mother and son. Her hair was a steel gray that she had braided into an intricate pattern. I figured if anyone might like the patterns my friend Jaycee created with her blown glass artwork, it would be this woman.

What likely passed for a smile in her mind made me think of the Queen of Hearts of Alice in Wonderland and the hiss from Delilah at my feet showed agreement. My feline familiar was a keen judge of character and I trusted her intuition as much as my own. Ray came quickly to my side, his dislike for the pair evident as the air cooled around us.

The woman tapped long, pointed fingernails that shone with a polish of deep purple atop my counter. "I don't suppose you'd have any antique pendants lying about? Anything with snakes?"

The young man rolled his eyes and pulled on her arm. They stepped away from the counter before I could answer and an awkward whispered argument ensued. I didn't mean to pry and so I bent to pick Delilah up and take her in back until the odd pair had left the shop. My witchy senses told me the woman's desire for an antique pendant with a snake motif wasn't coincidence, but I tried not to be paranoid and ignored the warning bells clanging in my head for now.

"Oh Miss," the woman's voice trilled from the front and I put Delilah on the chair by the table in back. Ray waited by the door but I knew he couldn't be convinced to leave me alone with my weird customers.

I focused on Delilah. "You wait right here until I can get rid of them. Then I'll send down to the Piggly Wiggly for some fresh salmon. My treat for leaving you so long while I went off into the woods." I scratched under her chin and hoped my offer would interest her.

"Coming," I called as I left my familiar and rushed back through the beaded curtains.

The woman looked triumphant as the man at her side seemed more agitated than before. She tapped one of her fingernails on my counter again as she peered down into the glass case below. "There! That's exactly what I was thinking of when we came in! I'd like that pendant right there."

The warning bells in my head turned to a shrieking siren as I looked down into the glass case that formed the base of my counter at the VV. I knew danged well I didn't have any pendants with a snake theme except the one in my pocket.

Eyes nearly popping out of my head, I bit my bottom lip hard to keep from shouting for Freddie. The pendant I knew had been in my pocket seconds ago rested front and center, against white velvet in a jeweler's box, right there in my case.

⬤ 6

Delilah's tail tickled my bare leg and I swallowed hard not even thinking to scold her for coming back up front. Keeping the shock I'd felt at seeing the pendant hidden as best I could, I looked up. The woman tapped her fingernails expectantly on the glass and her friend turned to walk away, mumbling to himself. Freddie and Sally came down in a rush then, their footsteps on the stairs loosing my tongue.

"I'm afraid to say it's not for sale, ma'am." I smiled in spite of my witchy senses going bonkers in my head.

"I don't understand," she complained, "why do you have it on display if it's not for sale?"

Her hand reached out to snatch her partner as she whined to me. The weird thing was, underlying that whiny tone was a note of undeniable steel. This woman was used to having her way no matter the price.

Freddie appeared at my side and deftly slid the glass door of the case open. His hand was on the pendant so quick, I almost missed the movement it made as he caught it when it lifted off its satin bed. "She can't sell something someone already bought, ma'am. My apologies, but this pendant is mine now."

The woman's face turned a bright red and I waited for the screams that were sure to follow. Instead, she smiled a big, wide fake smile. It was a horrible grimace, but at least she hadn't blown her top.

I watched as she warred with her emotions and the effect Freddie had on everyone who came in contact with him. Suddenly it was clear to me. This woman was a magickal being herself, and her partner was just a mortal, and a weasly one at that.

Freddie gave me a quick peck on the cheek before sweeping Sally to the back through the beaded curtains. I heard the back door slam shut behind them.

Letting loose a breath I hadn't known I was holding, I looked at the pair standing before my counter. The man was begging the woman to leave, but she eyed me with open hostility. "You shouldn't have sold that pendant to anyone else. You'll be sorry. I promise you that."

Squaring my shoulders, I let my own power run swiftly through my veins. I was amazed by the calm that the surge of mountain magick brought to me. "I'm not one to give threats or to be scared by them, ma'am. You best take your postcards and go."

She stared at me for a good long minute before throwing a five dollar bill on the counter and handing the postcards to the man who looked like he'd rather be roasting marshmallows in hell than standing another moment longer in my shop.

I felt the same as I watched the pair leave. Pulling out my cell phone, I dialed Freddie's number. I didn't want him leaving town until I knew what had happened to cause that pendant to leave my pocket and find its way into the display case.

The ringing of his phone echoed in the back room as he and Sally came back in from the alley. I was grateful they hadn't gone too far while I'd dispatched with the weird woman and her friend.

"Don't worry, we aren't going anywhere while that woman is in town," Freddie said as he and Sally came back up front.

"Who is she?" I asked, crestfallen that my friends couldn't leave Devil's Elbow.

"It's not who, but what. That pendant answers to

her and she's not here to help anybody we know, that's for sure. Something tells me she's mixed up in that murder out at the bed and breakfast." Freddie opened his hand and the pendant rose above his palm, levitating in the air. It moved toward the door of the VV on its own.

"For the love of Pete, what is that thing?" I cried as I moved to grab it out of the air. My booted feet scraped across the plank floor of the VV as the pendant pulled me along with it. If I hadn't seen it myself, I wouldn't have believed it.

Freddie moved to block the door before the pendant dragged me through it. Closing his hand over mine, he stopped the forward progress of the strange piece of jewelry. "She's a goblin, Jo. And this pendant is a relic she stole from someone far more powerful than any of us. I had to work a different spell real quick out there in the alley to keep her from tracking it until I can get it out of here."

Struggling to understand what my friend had just said, I marveled at his words. "A goblin? Aren't they trollish little creatures more apt to mischief than violence?"

My friend nodded. "For the most part, yes, but this one looks more like the redcaps that came over from Scotland centuries ago. Murderous lot they are.

And more dangerous than anything you've seen in these hills and hollers."

I hadn't picked up on exactly what the woman was when she was standing before me, but I didn't doubt Freddie. I'd heard of redcaps, and none of what I'd heard was good. They had no problem killing for what they desired.

"So you're saying that goblin, disguised as a woman, is after this pendant? But how did it end up at my cousin's bed and breakfast? The only guests that stayed there before the wedding were the magician, his assistant, and apparently his business manager."

Freddie took the pendant from my hand and wrapped it with some silk he pulled from his pocket. "My guess is that one of those three has some connection to the goblin. I called one of the elves of the Seelie Court who's still in the area to come and take this thing to our queen. It's not safe to keep it here where the goblin will kill to get their hands on it again."

A cold chill chased down my spine and I trembled as I thought of that goblin stalking my family and friends. "If the pendant is gone, y'all can take that trip and not worry about me. I've got my cousin, Delilah, and Aunt Dixie to watch out for me, and

Uncle Joe too. He's not going back to Flat Lick until later now."

Freddie looked at Sally and the two reluctantly agreed to take their trip. But the elf who was now related to me by marriage laid down the law. "We'll leave tomorrow morning first thing, but not before. By then, this pendant will be long gone and that goblin shouldn't bother you again."

Happy that the two of them would hang around Devil's Elbow for another night, I pulled my Jeep keys out of my pocket. "I know I just got back into town, but I'd like to go out and warn Billy Jack about this goblin and go by the Cumberland Gap jailhouse and see if there's anything I can do for Jessi, the magician's assistant."

Sally's brow furrowed as she moved closer to Freddie. "What's happened to Jessi? She's such a sweet girl and she saved the wedding supper entertainment without a fuss. She was actually really good, too."

I hadn't told them that Jessi was a suspect in the murder of the magician. Or that the two of them were romantically linked. Taking a moment to fill them in, I explained everything I knew. "She was the one standing over the body and holding the knife when we all came downstairs this morning. I don't think she did it, she told me she didn't, but stranger things have happened. Like that pendant and a goblin lurking around Devil's Elbow."

The drive back out to the bed and breakfast passed in a blur as I tried to work out the trouble we were all facing with a goblin in town and a murder on our hands. When I pulled up in the circular driveway at the bed and breakfast, Genie and Billy Jack were standing on the wide front porch holding hands. I found myself smiling from the inside out that Ray's baby sister had managed to tame my wild, lawless cousin.

No matter the challenges thrown their way, and there'd been a few noteworthy ones like djinn, demons, the Covey brothers and their crew, Ray and his grudging acceptance, and Billy Jack's moonshining habit, they'd made it through together. I was as sure of their future as I was that the sun would rise each day. It sounded cheesy, but love really could conquer all.

Climbing the steps, I breathed deeply, worried about the bad news I had to deliver. Neither of them really needed more on a day when everything had gone wrong.

We were in the midst of hugs when another car

came barreling down the driveway throwing gravel all over and raising a huge cloud of dust. I thought my eyes might pop clean out of my head when I saw who climbed out of the big SUV.

The goblin who'd wanted the pendant back at the VV threw open the driver's side door, her string of swear words lifting in the air and traveling up the porch to us before her foot even touched the bottom step. Her sidekick cowered in the car. I saw him flip the visor down to block the view of his goblin friend clomping up the steps to give us what-for.

If steam could actually come out of someone's ears, it would be pouring forth from the woman who stood before us blocking any way down the steps. I hadn't noticed in my shop, but the goblin lady seemed to fill whatever space she wished as an intimidation tactic.

My cousin wasn't the least bit pleased with the woman's sneering look cast at me and Genie. Billy Jack stepped forward protecting the two of us as the goblin's intentions were clear. She wasn't here on no social call.

"Excuse me, ma'am," he said so sweet that butter wouldn't melt in his mouth in spite of the way he flexed his muscles as he crossed his arms across his chest, "But we aren't open for business at the moment. I'd be happy to give you a card though, so you can call and book a room with us after we're officially open for business."

Genie and I peeked around Billy Jack as there was no peeking over his shoulder, broad as his back was. At once, I saw a glimpse of the goblin beneath the female veneer it wore but it was gone as soon as it appeared. By the way my cousin bristled as Genie's breathless squeak sounded from behind him, I knew he'd seen it too.

The woman grumbled out an answer to my cousin. "I'm not here to reserve a room, thank you very much. My husband was murdered here in your establishment this morning. I'm here to find out who did it and gather his belongings."

Shock that the magician had been married must have shown on my face. My mind went immediately to Jessi and whether she knew about this woman, and then whether the woman knew about Jessi. Things were about to boil over in the drama department. I honestly worried for Jessi's safety.

The deceased man's wife stuck out a hand to push my cousin aside and he growled low in his throat. It was a sound that would have stopped most any other magickal creature. We all knew when werewolves were ready to shred someone, but this goblin obviously didn't care one bit about the can of *behind whooping* my cousin was about to open on her.

The woman's partner, who'd stayed as silent as an empty grave at midnight, suddenly bolted out of the SUV and sprinted up onto the porch. "Please, sir. She's a grieving widow, you see. If you only let us in to collect his belongings, we'll make quick work of it and be out of your hair."

The goblin rounded on him and the fool had enough sense to fold faster than a cheap lawn chair as she swung her pocketbook at his head. "Arty!" she roared, her face flushing red as a ruby, "I done told you to keep your nose outta my bizness. You might have managed my husband's bizness, but you ain't managing mine. Git your narrow behind back in the car!"

So this pitiful, harangued man was Arty, the business manager Jessi told me about earlier. He'd been arguing with Roger the magician sometime before he was murdered. I wondered if the magician's missus knew that. Since I didn't want to see more blood spilled at my cousin's bed and breakfast, I zipped my lip about that piece of information. Jessi had told me in confidence after all. It was likely she'd told the police by now, too. Shoot! I needed to get down to the jailhouse to see about her.

Billy Jack was in no mood to entertain the pair. When he took hold of the goblin's arm and guided her back down the steps, I focused all my energy and readied a spell that would help contain the prickly woman. Not knowing how powerful, or vicious, this particular goblin was, I didn't want to take any chances.

To my surprise, she didn't try to kill any of us right off the bat. Billy Jack tried to reason with her, but the edge in his voice was a clear warning that he wouldn't hesitate to eliminate a threat, even if that threat appeared to be a lady. "I'm so sorry for your loss, ma'am, but the police here in Cumberland Gap have his possessions, the magic props and all. You'll have to see them to make the claim as his wife. Please accept our condolences," he stopped and looked back at Genie. She stepped down off the porch onto the next step, her feet failing her as she halted in going any further.

Arty, much to his credit, took hold of the goblin's other arm and gently led her away. "Come on now, Sheila. Leave these good people alone. They didn't have nothing to do with this mess."

The magician's wife wheeled around and pointed at me. "Well she was no help earlier! Giving that pendant to that filthy elf in her musty old shop."

"She was only sellin' running her business. We'll talk to the elf if we can find him and see if he'll sell it to us. He didn't seem to be a bad feller. Let's go claim Roger's things and head back to Devil's Elbow. I just know we can fix all this." Arty pleaded convincingly with the goblin, all the while pulling the reluctant creature closer to the SUV.

I was fairly jumping with the magickal energy I'd called forth and so when the two of them piled back inside the vehicle and peeled off back down the driveway, I was plumb wore out and sweating like a pig. Genie came back up on the porch and led me inside. "Come on Jo. You need some of my huckleberry sweet tea. Aunt Dixie taught me her recipe and I added a little something extra to make it my own. It'll fix you right up."

Billy Jack came bounding up the steps behind us. "What do you know about those two, Jo? Gettin' on the wrong side of a goblin ain't the smartest thing I've ever seen you do."

7

It had taken me the better part of an hour, and two glasses of huckleberry sweet tea, to explain everything I knew to my cousin and Genie. By the time I finally left them, the afternoon was turning to evening. As soon as I'd sat down with Billy Jack and Genie, I had called Freddie at the VV to warn him the goblin was on her way back to Devil's Elbow. He'd agreed to close the shop since I wasn't going to be back until after supper time.

I'd apologized to him, and as was his way, he'd told me not to worry. "Elves are the best friends you could have right now, Jo. We aren't afraid of goblins and best of all, we're the only magickal creatures they respect. I couldn't leave y'all at the mercy of this creature."

As I pulled away from the bed and breakfast, I

was grateful for my friend. When we'd first met up in Louisville at the Appalachian Baking Contest, I knew he was something special. He'd proved his loyalty to my family time and time again and I meant to see that he and Sally got the break they deserved from the drama of being in our inner circle.

Driving the winding back roads of Cumberland Gap brought back memories of my teenage years. Genie had been much too young for the shenanigans Ray, Billy Jack, and I got up to back then. Mrs. Davis would have skinned us alive if we'd taken her to the falls with us. I still couldn't believe any of us had made it to adulthood in one piece the way we risked our lives at Cumberland Falls in the pursuit of good fun on the sunny, lazy days of summer.

Ray appeared in the seat beside me, his grin as big as my own. He was thinking the same thing as me. "You know, we could make a trip to the falls this evening after you see Jessi."

I liked that idea. It would be a romantic break from the unending weirdness of the day. But first I wanted to know what he'd been up to while I was at the bed and breakfast. "So, tell me where you went after the goblin left the VV."

My ghostly fiancee whistled softly to the country song on the Jeep radio. I glanced over at him, surprised to see the wind moving his hair, ruffling it and making it seem like he was alive and well next to me. I swallowed the mix of emotions that surged through me. Soon we would marry like we'd always planned. That assurance lifted my mood and I waited patiently for his reply knowing we'd go out to the falls after I saw Jessi.

"I wanted to see if Deputy Carter knew anything about this goblin or her buddy and so I went to see him at the courthouse. After I described the two, he recalled pullin' them over out on Trunk Road yesterday evening. Seems their SUV was weavin' all over the road but neither one of them was drinkin'. They'd been fussin' with each other, though. He gave the woman a ticket and she wasn't real happy about that. He said since she was a goblin, and since he hadn't seen her around before, he was keepin' an eye out on his patrols around town."

I wondered why Arty, the magician's business manager, was arguing with his boss's wife, and riding around Devil's Elbow with her to boot. And where had the missus been all this time?

Billy Jack told me that the magician, Jessi, and Arty had checked in three days before the wedding. He'd never seen the goblin before and said Jessi and Roger were pretty tight in spite of having separate rooms at the bed and breakfast. I turned down the radio and glanced over at Ray. "There's a whole lot wrong with this entire situation. It seems Jessi and the wife may not have known about each other and the business manager was arguing with both the magician and his wife. Deputy Carter caught one argument and Jessi caught the other. I'm beginnin' to think there was something rotten at the core of the magician's personal life. Probably why he was drinkin' so bad the night of the wedding."

"And probably why he was stabbed to death. Very rarely is anyone killed by a random stranger," Ray replied, his eyes on the road ahead.

"Well, that's true except for the people we know. Like the set up to pin a murder on my cousin at his still site. And poor Melba Hoskins, her killer was basically a stranger to her. And Maybelle, she didn't know…"

Ray held up a hand to stop me. "Most people know their killers. It seems in our circle, outside forces often cause mayhem and skew the data. With this case, it would appear there are lots of juicy details that might prove my hunch to be true."

I couldn't argue his point. The magician had been using Jessi, arguing with his manager, and apparently cheating on his wife. Any one of them could have snapped on him and committed a crime of passion. The question was, how did the onyx snake pendant figure into it all?

Even the thought of moonlight skinnydipping at Cumberland Falls with Ray couldn't dispel the tangle of worry gathering in my chest. We only had a few days before opening weekend at the bed and breakfast. If I could prove it was someone the magician knew and not someone connected to my cousin's business, I'd do whatever it took to help Genie and Billy Jack.

The inside of the jailhouse in the Gap was a basic beige with speckled tile floors and a drop ceiling sporting depressing fluorescent lighting. There were a few clerks scattered around the room, each busy with a different task.

I hoped I wasn't too late for visiting hours and that they'd even let me see Jessi since I wasn't a relation or her lawyer. I figured if it came to it, I could always use an enchantment spell to get my way. Of course, I didn't like doing it, but it would be cast in an effort to help my friend so it wasn't so bad after all.

A tall deputy came into the front area and I gave a quick wave when he looked my way. As the man came closer, I recognized him immediately. "Chase Fuson, is that you? I didn't know you were a law man now!"

"Well, I'll be! If it ain't *the* Jolene Baker. It sure is good to see you." He came through the swinging doors that separated the clerks from the row of wooden chairs in the waiting area. Before I could get another word out, he grabbed me up in his arms for a big old bear hug. Ray cleared his throat loudly and I laughed.

Chase was a wolf shifter with the Gap pack and I wondered if he could see or hear Ray. My question was answered when he turned to my boyfriend and gave him a wide grin. He kept his voice low so the mortal clerks didn't overhear him. "I'm glad to see you too Ray Davis! Even if you are among the dearly departed. I knew Jo wasn't about to let you go on to your eternal rest when I heard about your accident."

I was a little surprised Chase saw Ray, but ever since I'd gotten my soul streak from visiting Ray through astral travel, more and more magickal folks could see him. I'd definitely done something to him that might come back to bite me. Pushing away those unpleasant thoughts, I addressed the other unpleasant topic that had brought me to the jail-house. "So Chase, I'm here to see your suspect in the murder of that magician over at my cousin's bed and breakfast. Am I too late for visiting hours?"

He glanced down at the watch on his wrist and his eyebrows lifted in surprise. "I reckon you'd be pushin' it, Jolene. But since we're old friends, and since I'd hate to see Billy Jack's new business venture suffer bad press, I can take you back. You know, back in the day I used to bootleg your cousin's 'shine for him. Has he really gone straight and stopped 'shining altogether?"

I knew his question was one a lot of our friends and neighbors would ask if they had the chance. It was still hard for me to believe and I'd had some of Billy Jack's legal apple brandy and tasted some of his hard cider and craft beers. He sure did have a talent for home brew. Shrugging, I shared my thoughts with the lanky deputy. "It's hard to think of Devil's Elbow without my cousin's moonshine, and believe me, there's folks still tryin' to get him to run one more batch of mash. But Genie's changed him for the better. He's taken to home brewing like a fish to water. You ought to stop by and taste what he's got on tap."

Ray lifted his arm and tapped his finger on his wrist. "Time's a wastin', y'all."

Chase turned and pushed open one of the swinging doors he'd come through and held it for me as I walked past him. "Which suspect you hopin' to see, Jo?"

Stopping in my tracks, I turned with a confused look on my face. "I thought you only had the one, my friend Jessi, the magician's assistant. You mean to tell me there's another suspect?"

My voice was hopeful because if there was another suspect, Jessi had a chance of being cleared of suspicion of murder.

"We had the magician's manager come in with the widow a little while ago. She was somethin' else, I tell you," he leaned close and lowered his voice again like before, "I think she might be magickal, but I couldn't figure it out. I can't say why we took him in and booked him, but the magician's wife was awful mad about it. She wanted to post bail right then and there, but that's not how things work around here. She huffed off in a snit after throwing a hissy fit for the ages."

They must have come right over to claim the magician's personal effects after they left the bed and breakfast. I sure was glad I'd missed that little scene. Having had more than enough of the goblin, I waited for Chase to lead me back to the cell where they were holding Jessi. As we passed through the thick metal door that led to the holding area and the actual cell block, it struck me that I ought to talk to Arty the business manager while I was there, if he would agree to see me.

8

Jessi was sitting on the metal bunk in her cell that was outfitted with a thin mattress. My heart went out to her as she hopped up and dropped the paperback she'd been reading when she saw it was me who had come to see her.

"Jolene! I knew you'd come. I'm as happy as a dog with two tails considering my surroundings." She lifted a hand to gesture at her cell.

Deputy Fuson left us with the admonition that we had all of fifteen minutes before he returned to see me out. I hadn't bothered him about Arty just yet, I wanted to speak with Jessi before asking just in case it made him regret helping me.

"So," I said as I turned to face her through the bars, "this can't be easy, cooped up here and accused of murderin' someone you loved."

Jessi twisted a strand of her blonde hair between her fingers and sighed. Her eyelids were rimmed red and the dried tears on her cheeks showed though she'd tried to swipe them away. Her voice wavered at first as she began to speak. "I'm beginning to wonder if he loved me. Turns out he has a wife he forgot to mention."

As she finished, her voice had grown angry and laced with bitter resentment. I wished there weren't bars between us because the poor woman needed a hug, at least.

"How'd you find that out? I mean I just found out earlier today and let me tell you, she's none too pleasant. Hopefully she doesn't know about your relationship with her husband."

I doubted that the goblin did know about the role Jessi had played in her husband's personal life. If she'd found out about that, my friend would likely be missing instead of standing before me and the Cumberland Gap jail would have been a smoking heap of bricks.

"Well, I saw Arty when they marched him past to the men's cell block and he didn't say so much as boo, mind you. The deputy that just brought you back was talking to the other policeman back here about how Roger's wife was causing a ruckus over Arty's arrest.

Said they were afraid she might bring the roof down around them."

"I would say your secret is safe for now and that having Arty as a suspect is also good news on your part. At least they have someone else to investigate. Is there anything I can bring you in here or anyone I can contact for you?"

Jessi smiled and pushed her hair back from her face. "They let me have a few calls but I sure ain't got a lawyer. That's not something I'd ever thought I might need. Do you know of any in the area who might take my case? The public defender they promised hasn't been here yet so I don't know how that's gonna work out."

Obviously she'd already talked to the police without the benefit of legal representation or they wouldn't have known that Arty was with Roger after Jessi left him on the deck. I thought I might advise her to zip her lip until I talked to Uncle Joe. We could always ask Granny's lawyer. "Listen, I believe you're innocent but until you hear from me again, plead the fifth with the police on any further questions. I'm hoping you haven't told them about your relationship with Roger?"

She shook her head in denial. "That's the last thing I'd ever tell them willingly. I'm already in enough trouble as it is. But Arty sure might tell them."

Chase's voice echoed down the hallway and I placed a finger to my lips to silence Jessi. She stuck a hand through the bars and I took hold of it. "Thank you, Jolene. I really do appreciate you comin' down here to see me. I'll think about what you've said. Come back as soon as you can, you hear?"

I squeezed her hand and smiled. Chase came up behind me and Jessi pulled her hand back through the iron bars between us. I waved goodbye as I followed Chase to a desk further down the hallway past Jessi's cell.

"You have to sign the log book as a visitor for Miss Jessi before you go, Jolene. Strictly policy, you know." His warm smile and larger than life shifter presence was so out of place in the gray nondescript hallway. It eased my mind a little to know that Jessi would have someone as kind as Chase on duty for her first night in jail. He handed me the pen and I recalled wanting to see Arty.

"You know, I think I might need to see the magician's business manager too. He was awful nice to my family while he was staying at the bed and breakfast. I can't believe he's a murderer."

Chase eyed me as I tried to keep a straight face. I hated lying to anyone, especially a friend, but desperate times called for such measures. Hoping my eyes conveyed innocence instead of deception, I smiled encouragingly at him.

He rolled his eyes before turning to lead me down the hallway to see Arty. I took a moment to squeeze his arm and smile up at him as we stopped before the cell that held the business manager. "Thanks Chase, I won't be but a minute, I promise. I only want to give him a good word since he was so kind to my cousin."

Arty seemed leery of me after Chase left us and I was glad he hadn't showed his hesitancy to my friend.

"Hey Arty!" I said as cheerily as I could. Feeling like a total faker, I gave a little wave and smiled.

Arty wasn't as thrilled as Jessi had been to see me, but he did come closer to the bars and peer at me. "Aren't you that lady at The Value Vintage who sold that pendant right out from under Sheila?"

Deciding to go with it since he'd seen me plainly and knew the name of my shop, I nodded. "That's me. I heard they'd arrested you when you showed up here with the magician's missus. I hoped you might tell me what that pendant means to her. I have a feeling she'd do anything to have it in her hands."

He gave a chuckle that held very little mirth. "You're not wrong, I'll give you that. I feel like you should know I didn't kill Roger. He was my good friend. I kept every secret he ever had and then some. But his wife, Sheila, she'll move heaven and earth to get that pendant. It's hers, that much I know for certain. But it's best she never gets it back."

Chase came jogging back to the cell and took me by the arm before I could say another word to Arty. "You gotta go, Jolene. I'm about to face the wrath of the sheriff if he sees you back here."

I was irritated and not the least bit cooperative. I dug my heels in, but my shifter friend was far too strong for my resistance to make any difference. "But he'll see my name in your logbook, dontcha' think?"

That caught him up short as we stopped at the desk where his logbook and pen rested on a desk blotter. I knew he wasn't gonna make me sign it and that was good news. "Never mind all that. You're going out the back. I swear if you tell anyone you were here or that I let you back, we are no longer friends. And you wouldn't want that."

I didn't have a leg to stand on and he danged well knew it. Knowing Chase had stuck his neck out for me and done me a solid, I relented. Before I disappeared out the back door, I got up on my tiptoes and kissed his cheek. "Thanks, Chase. You're just like the brother I never had."

Ray came up behind us and gave Chase a shove with his shoulder. "You heard her, son. You're in the brother zone. Tuck your tongue back in your mouth, young pup. She's mine."

I giggled at Ray and his protective behavior. I couldn't blame him since Chase and every other man in these hills and hollers had the advantage of a beating heart in their chest. But Ray had my heart and that was all that really mattered.

In spite of the brief encounters with both Jessi and Arty, I felt like the information they'd given me was valuable. More questions swirled in my head as I waited for Ray to join me in the alley beside the jailhouse. I needed to know why the pendant was so important to the goblin, well beside the fact that it was an ancient relic. Most any magickal creature would want to possess such a powerful artifact. And what about Jessi? She'd quickly told the police about Arty and his arguments with Roger, but she hadn't said a peep about her own relationship with the man.

As much as I wanted to believe Jessi, I knew I couldn't count her out as the murderer. She might have known about Sheila long before today and pulled one over on me.

Ray's hands on my shoulders pulled me out of my thoughts and I sighed as he wrapped an arm around me and led me back down the alley toward the parking lot across from the jailhouse. "We still goin' down to the falls for some skinnydipping, babe?"

His eyes were filled with lustful hope and I laughed, happy to see the old Ray coming through perfectly clear in his intent.

"I reckon it would be the perfect ending to this stressful day." I pulled at my tank top as I realized I was sweaty and sticky from the heat rising off the pavement. The cool water at the bottom of the falls would feel like heaven and a fleeting naughty thought of being under water with Ray made me smile with anticipation.

Once we were in the Jeep, I turned up the radio and sang all the way to the trailhead at the top of the falls. The moon was full and I pointed it out to Ray. "I bet we get to see a moonbow tonight!"

"Oh, I'm going to see more than the moon or a moonbow tonight, hot stuff," he growled as he pulled me into his embrace for a sweet, long kiss.

The falls drowned out the world around us and the noise soothed me as Ray's kisses made me long for the days we came here in our youth as a goofy, teen-aged couple in love.

When he'd had enough of my lips, I led him down the trail with a contingent of fireflies I'd called to me just for the purpose of helping us to see our way in the dusk of twilight. It was romantic to say the least.

At the bottom of the trail, we hurried down along the river bank until we found our favorite spot. It was far enough away to see the falls in all their glory as they tumbled endlessly over the edge of the sandstone ledge, but the water was calmer and perfect for skinnydipping. As I shucked my clothes and ran headlong into the water, Ray came after me, his form gliding effortlessly through the water. I envied how he could sail across without disturbing the sandy bottom.

Coming up for air, another thing Ray had no need to worry about, I gasped as the vision of a moonbow appeared in the mist from the falls. Ray rose out of the water behind me, his form warm against the chilled ripples dancing across my skin.

"I'd say the falls are happy to see us," Ray whispered as he trailed his lips along the beads of water on my left shoulder.

Sighing happily, I turned away from the beautiful moonbow and thanked Mother Earth and our Heavenly Father for their bounty and for the gift of Ray Dang Davis.

9

Ray and I had pitched a tent down by the falls after our romantic swim and my morning alarm was the lovely sound of birdsong nearby. It had to be perched on a branch right outside for me to hear it over the falls and if my ears didn't fail me, it was a cardinal welcoming the day.

Zipping out of my sleeping bag, I shook out my clothes and pulled them on as I shivered a little from the cool air that still lingered along the river bank. Ray was not beside me and so I figured he was already wandering the woods or waiting in the Jeep for me.

Taking down the tent was easier than pie and soon, I had all my things packed up and ready to tote back up the trail. My cell phone battery was low and I only glanced at my notifications as I pulled a granola bar out of my backpack. Genie had called the night before and I hoped all was well at the bed and breakfast. Tapping on the phone screen, I pressed the device against my ear as I moved into the woods away from the falls.

"Good morning, Jo," Genie greeted me and I could tell that she was much happier today than yesterday. "I probably called you too late last night, but Billy Jack wants to have a little barbecue out here tonight for a small group of friends and family to take his mind off the magician. You and Ray will come by, I hope?"

My stomach rumbled at the thought of barbecue two nights in a row and I laughed. "We wouldn't miss it. Freddy and Sally are on the guest list too, right?"

Since he was now our relation by marriage, I figured we ought to include him in family gatherings as often as we could. Plus, it would soothe my guilt about the two of them having to postpone their trip to Dollywood.

"I called this morning and invited them. I was just about to call you since they said you hadn't come home last night. Freddy sounded worried about you, you should call him after we hang up. He was worried about that goblin that came by the VV yesterday. I told him we'd had our own run-in with her." Genie's earlier enthusiasm faded a little as she spoke of the magician's wife.

Thoughts of that wild card brought the equivalent of dark clouds to my own mind. "I should have called him last night, but me and Ray were having too good of a time out here at Cumberland Falls."

Genie gasped and then giggled. "It was a nice night for skinnydippin'."

My face heated immediately at her guess. I wasn't quick enough to dispel her notion and her laughter drifted across the digital device in my hand.

"Possum pellets! I'm not gonna kiss and tell, Genie Davis! But it sounds like you and my cousin might have done the same thing out at your pond."

"I can neither confirm nor deny, but since you and Ray like the falls, maybe I can get Billy Jack to take me there this summer," Genie gushed, her laughter causing my lips to lift in a genuine smile. Her joy was infectious.

"He'll know all the best spots since we used to come out here all the time in high school. But yeah, count us in for the barbecue. It'll be nice to have something good goin' on at the bed and breakfast again. You need me to bring anything?"

Genie's voice was muffled for a moment and I heard my cousin's bass in the background. She was back on the line in a few seconds without missing a beat. "Nope, nothing but my brother. We've got leftovers from the wedding supper and you know how good barbecue is the second day. We'll see y'all tonight!"

We hung up and I found Freddie's number quick as a whip. As I waited for him to answer, I bit off a piece of granola bar and chewed methodically. Noting that it was time to replenish my stash due to the stale taste of the oats, I swallowed quickly when Freddie answered. His voice sounded like he was irritated.

"Hey friend! I'm sorry I didn't call and let you know where we were last night, but time got away from me. Can you forgive me for worryin' you?" I pleaded sweetly as I turned and walked back through the woods to the riverbank.

I saw Ray standing by the tent gear and waved. On the phone, Freddie sighed. "There's nothing to forgive, my friend. That goblin just has me on edge. I'm happy to report that the pendant was given to the Seelie Queen a few hours ago so that's something to help ease our minds."

"That does make a huge difference, Freddie, thank you! Now you and Sally can go on and head out for Dollywood, after the barbecue tonight, that is."

Freddie tried to list all the reasons he shouldn't go, but I reminded him that my rather formidable aunt and uncle were in Devil's Elbow, and Billy Jack was only a few miles away. His doubt melted and I heard the stress leave his voice as he told me to come on home. Pleased that all was well at the VV, I hung up and shoved my cell phone into my back pocket.

Ray hugged me tight and kissed my forehead as I lifted my small tent, that I'd secured in it's old, army green duffel, off the ground. He frowned as I looked up. "You ready to go back to the real world, Jo?"

Sighing, I kissed his lips with fervor but kept the affectionate contact shorter than I liked. "I wish we could live here by the river on love and moonbows, but I really need to give Freddie and Sally a break. After the barbecue tonight, they'll finally head off to Dollywood for a few days."

He followed me as I made my way back to the trail that led up the hill to the top of the falls. "Then we'll have the VV all to ourselves and live on love and the memory of moonbows there. Did he mention the goblin at all?"

"He said the pendant was with the Seelie Queen, which means that particular person shouldn't bother us again. And even if she does, Uncle Joe and Aunt Dixie are close at hand. I'm more worried about who killed Roger the magician."

We worked our way up the hill slowly and I grumbled about how much easier it was going down than it was coming back up. Ray lamented the fact that he was unable to help me with my burden.

When we got to the parking lot, he pointed at the Jeep. A weird green cloud dissipated from around my vehicle. I blinked my eyes twice wondering if I was just seeing things or if it was a trick of the mist from the falls. "What in the world?" I whispered as I dropped my gear on the ground.

I was about to sprint for the Jeep when Ray floated in front of me. "Stay back, Jo. Let me check this out. Somethin' ain't right."

Looking around the parking lot, I didn't see any other vehicles or even any other people out and about. It was pretty early on a weekday morning for anyone else to be out at the falls, even though it was summer. Most campers would be settled further down the river at the campground with RV hook-ups.

In spite of the fact it was daylight out, I felt goosebumps up and down my arms. That green cloud had been ominous to say the least and downright freaky. I couldn't completely shake the feeling that my Jeep was tampered with on purpose.

Picking up my backpack and the duffel that held my tent, I waited impatiently for Ray to return to my side. Shading my eyes, I watched as he circled around the Jeep, went in and came back out the front passenger door and then moved around the front and crawled beneath the tires. I could see from where I stood that my beloved vehicle sat a little kitty-cornered.

When Ray came back to me, we both stated the obvious in unison. "Flat tires."

I blew out a frustrated breath and dragged myself over to inspect the damage. Kneeling down, I saw that someone or something had slashed the front and rear passenger side tires. It wasn't the work of someone with a knife, that was for sure. These marks looked like something with claws had torn through the sturdy rubber tires and scratched the rims.

"I think you best work some magick my witchy woman, or else you'll be hiking back to town this mornin'," Ray advised as I moved to the back of the Jeep and loaded my stuff inside.

"You're right. I only have one spare and I need to get back to Devil's Elbow so Freddie and Sally don't have to open the VV. I suppose it's using my magick to help them as well as myself."

Ray rolled his eyes at me and went to sit in the passenger seat while I worked my spell on the two tires. I thought about erasing the claw marks on the tires and the rims as my magick mended them, but at the last second I saved their imprints for Uncle Joe to inspect. I'd feel better if he knew what happened and could weigh in on the matter.

"Come on sunshine," Ray called as he leaned out the window and smiled at me, his face as handsome as ever and coming through clear as day.

"You're awfully happy for someone whose girl-friend's ride was just vandalized by a strange green cloud," I groused as I walked around the front of the Jeep pulling the keys from my pocket.

"Vandalized by a goblin more like it," he replied as I buckled myself into the driver's seat.

"Don't say that!" The goosebumps from earlier returned with a vengeance and I felt the hairs on the nape of my neck stand up. Turning the key, I revved the engine and shoved it into drive, peeling out of the parking lot with a little more drama than was neces-sary. It felt good to leave the wooded area behind and fly down the paved road toward home.

As we passed the county line separating Cumber-land Gap and Devil's Elbow, I looked at Ray. "Don't you dare tell Freddie or Sally about the tires. They won't leave town if you do. Whatever happened, even if it was the magician's missus, my family will handle it, okay?"

Ray hesitated. "I don't hold with lying, Jo, and you dang well know it."

I gave him a mean side-eye. "It ain't lying if you don't say nothing, Ray. What they don't know won't hurt them. The pendant is gone and the goblin could have done a whole lot worse than give me two flat tires. We were all alone on the riverbank all night, remember?"

He sighed and shook his head. "Well, I won't have you in that kind of situation again while that woman, or thing, is runnin' loose all over the creation. From here on out, you're always with one of us. Either me, or Dixie, or Joe, or even Billy Jack. Wait," he said, lifting his hand, "scratch that last one. I don't want my baby sister in harm's way. And I know danged well she will be if that goblin is after you. We have to steer clear of the bed and breakfast till this murder is solved."

"Okay. I'll leave it to you to tell your little sister we ain't comin' to her barbecue tonight. That oughta be fun." I knew he wouldn't pay a call on Genie and upset her plans. His face revealed that he knew that I knew that he knew he wouldn't do any such thing, either.

Smiling, I flicked on the radio and laughed before belting out Dolly's famous ballad about always loving you on the local country music station.

Ray hollered over the noise. "You ain't right, Jolene. You know that?"

10

The lights were on in Aunt Dixie's bakery as I pulled into my spot in front of the VV. That granola bar I'd half eaten back at Cumberland Falls had done a poor job of staving off my hunger pains and so I happily left my gear and my grouchy ghost in the Jeep.

When I let myself in the front door with my master key, I was the landlord after all and ownership had its privileges, I called out to my aunt and hustled behind the bakery counter. The smell of fresh dough, cinnamon, lemon, and cherry crowded my nostrils and I breathed it all in deeply. My stomach nearly strangled me in its urgency to eat all the carbs my nose was telling it were at hand. It wasn't my fault the two conspired to add pounds to my frame.

"Aunt Dixie! You got any scraps for a poor orphan girl back there?" I laughed as I rounded the corner to the kitchen where my aunt's ovens were already working overtime.

My aunt bopped around the room with a mixing bowl resting against her hip while she sang into a wooden spoon that hadn't yet made it's way into the bowl.

For a minute, I thought her hips might send that bowl flying as she swished around the counter. I could see the fancy ear pods I'd bought for her birthday last year had finally been put to good use. Aunt Dixie didn't despise technology, she was just slow to adopt it. Especially since wifi signals in and around Devil's Elbow worked about as good as an old hound dog on a sunny front porch.

I crossed my arms and waited for her to open her eyes and find me standing before her. There wasn't any way I could keep from startling her, so I planted my feet and grinned at the carefree way she moved closer to me.

About the time she saw me, Ray tapped on my shoulder and we both nearly jumped out of our skin. I placed a hand over my heart as the incident at the falls still had me on edge.

"You two! Ain't you ever heard of knockin' first?" Aunt Dixie pulled her ear pods out and gave us both what-for.

Ray was laughing at the both of us, not the least

bit bothered by the set down my aunt was fixing to deliver.

I, on the other hand, displayed my good manners and excellent home training. "I'm sorry, Aunt Dixie! I did call out as I came in and I locked the door behind me, but apparently some people have boundary issues."

Shooting a smug look at Ray, I held out my open arms for my aunt to give me the customary hug she always did whenever I came over to see about her. This time, I was left standing with my arms out in front of me.

"Lord, I'm busy as a long-tailed cat in a room full of rockin' chairs! Is it any chance you've come home from the woods for good so I can have Sally back full time?" Aunt Dixie plopped her mixing bowl on the counter and stared at me.

Letting my arms drop, I pulled a sad face hoping for forgiveness. "Well, I hate to tell you that she and Freddie are headed off to Dollywood first thing tomorrow mornin', but maybe she can come down today?"

My aunt was not impressed. Her scowl was fierce. "You young'uns will be the death of me someday, I swan! Now, either tie on an apron and make yourself useful or go fetch Sally here to me. With my brother stayin' upstairs with them fellers he calls a band, there's a ton of biscuits to be made."

She went over to one of her ovens that dinged out a warning from its timer and pulled the door open. Two huge cast iron skillets waited to be placed on the trivets sitting all around her butcher block island that sat smack in the middle of the bakery kitchen.

Aunt Dixie hefted them out without missing a beat and I drooled over the buttery tops that were kissed a light golden brown. Gingerly reaching for one, I juggled it from hand to hand since it was still as hot as Hades.

"You could have waited five minutes, child," Aunt Dixie said as she put a whole skillet on a plate and handed it to me.

"I love you!" I gushed as I leaned closer to her and kissed her rosy cheek with a loud smack of my lips.

She smiled just a little and I laughed. "Git on outta here and don't come back without Sally. I really need her today."

Ray made himself useful as he inhaled the fresh biscuit steam coming from my plate. "I'll go get her for you. Jolene needs to tell you what happened out at the falls this morning."

A gruff voice rang out at the rear of the kitchen. "What was y'all doin' at the falls this mornin'?"

Uncle Joe waltzed on into the kitchen, his eyes

pinning me so I couldn't escape with Ray. My boyfriend was already gone, though. I bet he'd seen Uncle Joe standing in the back before he even opened his spectral mouth about the falls.

Aunt Dixie plated the other skillet of biscuits and moved to the next oven that was dinging out its status. "What do you think they was doin' out there, Joe? Countin' crawdads? You ain't the only romantic in town."

Uncle Joe and I stared at Aunt Dixie as she plated two more skillets worth of biscuits. Well wasn't she just full of sass and vinegar this morning? I shook my head and bit into my biscuit, not waiting to put honey or butter or grape jelly on it.

My uncle took a biscuit from my plate and I slapped at his hand. "No you don't, get your own plate mister."

He ignored me and bit into the one he'd managed to pilfer because, as a shifter, his reflexes were much faster than mine. Aunt Dixie shoved a plate into his hands and turned to stare at me. "Go on and tell your tale, child. We ain't got all day, you know. I'm gonna have to open in less than an hour after feeding your uncle's *band*."

The way Aunt Dixie put the emphasis on that last word made me giggle but Uncle Joe ignored the barb. Instead, he pulled up a stool and sat down with his biscuits, reaching for the grape jelly Aunt Dixie had sitting out just for all us biscuit eaters.

"Now short stack, git to tellin' us what happened out at the falls. PG parts only please." He laughed at his little joke and I rolled my eyes before pulling up a stool beside him.

"How does a goblin slashin' my tires strike you, Uncle Joe? That's about as PG as it gets, I'm afraid."

Dropping his biscuit on his plate, my uncle looked at me like I had a second head growing out of my neck. His expression quickly changed from shock to alarm. "I'm gonna to assume you ain't pulling my leg, niece. I really hope you're not pulling my leg cause that's something that could give your old uncle a heart attack if it's true."

I glanced over at Aunt Dixie. She'd stopped dead in her tracks and stood with a skillet of biscuits in each hand as the timers dinged all around us. I shoved Uncle Joe and we both hopped up to help empty the ovens of their precious, buttery goodness.

"Jolene, I swan if you're tryin' to pull the wool on your uncle, I'll tan your hide right here and now! Talk of goblins ain't funny, young lady and I don't need that kind of aggravation." Aunt Dixie had managed to put her skillets safely on the counter but her brows were drawn together in supreme agitation.

I tried to soothe them both but the cat was out of

the bag. "I'm not lyin' or trying to pull anyone's leg. It seems that the magician who was murdered out at The Drunken Rooster was married to a goblin. And she's here lookin' for a relic that Freddie sent to the Seelie Queen by way of his fellow elves in order to keep me safe."

My aunt and uncle looked at each other like I'd lost my mind. It was a good minute before either of them could form enough of a thought to make a sentence, but boy, when they did, they fell all over each other as they peppered me with questions.

"Why didn't you tell us?"

"Why would you take yourself out to the falls alone with a goblin huntin' you down?"

"What were you thinkin' letting Freddie send the relic to the Seelie Queen?"

"I thought Ray Davis had better sense than to allow such a foolish thing as campin' out at the lake with danger like that at your door. I know he's a ghost, but has he lost his mind too?"

I held up a hand and shoved another biscuit in my mouth, not caring that grape jelly dribbled down my chin.

Uncle Joe picked up a napkin and wiped it off like I was five years old again. Which honestly is how I felt with the two of them displaying their displeasure at the actions of me and my friends.

They stared at me until I finished chewing my biscuit.

"Okay," I began, my voice revealing my sudden attack of nerves, "maybe we didn't make the best choices here, but the goblin only slashed my tires. She surely had plenty of time to cut the brake line or attack me in my tent. I think she just wants to scare me."

I hadn't consciously rationalized the whole event at the falls until that moment, but it made sense. Ray had known there was no real danger to us as soon as he finished his survey of the damage, otherwise he would have hustled me into the car while he did recon. I let out a long slow breath of relief.

Aunt Dixie placed her hands on her hips and shook her head. "You don't know that for sure, Jolene. You just want to believe it and I can't say as how I blame you. But you better get it through your head that a goblin, and a female one to boot, is nothing to play with."

"She's right. And I'm stuck to you like glue from here on out. My band can stay here and I'll bunk on your couch for the time being. Let's git on down to the VV so I can do some recon on the place. That goblin is wrong as two left shoes if she thinks she can just waltz into Devil's Elbow and mess with my family." Uncle Joe grabbed a to-go bag off the counter behind him and shoved his biscuits inside.

I followed suit and mumbled my apologies to them both. "I guess I just didn't think she'd bother me after the pendant was gone. But please, don't tell Freddie or Sally. They won't leave for their little trip if they think I might get hurt. Promise? I'll do whatever you say without a bit of sass."

Aunt Dixie hustled us out the back door and kissed my cheek. "I'll keep my mouth shut about it this time 'cause them two sure do need to get away for awhile. They both took real good care of the VV and of Delilah for you."

"Thanks, Aunt Dixie! What would I do without you?"

She laughed and swarped at me with her dish towel as I skipped away. "You'd starve child, that's what all y'all would do without me!"

"You ain't wrong, Dixie!" Uncle Joe hollered back down the alley as he popped another biscuit in his mouth.

The barbecue at The Drunken Rooster was in full swing by the time me, Ray, and my Uncle Joe arrived. I waved at Sally, who I hadn't seen since earlier that day when she hurried down to the bakery to help Aunt Dixie. She and Freddie held matching red cups that they lifted in welcome as I approached.

Uncle Joe thankfully relaxed his watch over me once someone hollered out asking him and his Shifty River Boys to play something over by the bonfire out past the grill. Billy Jack hopped up from his seat between Zeke and Floyd to grab Genie by the hand before bellowing out a request for *their* song so they could dance.

The simple things in life always made me happy, even when I was worried about the bad times. Freddie touched my arm and I turned to see that

Sally had left us and I knew something was bothering my friend. "What's wrong, Freddie?"

He stared at me, his gaze not allowing me to look away. "What's wrong, Jo? You know you can't hide much from me."

"Hey, it's not fair to use your elf powers on me like that, you know." Trying to put him off so I could see if he'd heard about my flat tires, I chose the tactic of distraction.

His chuckle proved I couldn't waylay the conversation. "I don't need my powers when my eyes see well enough."

Sticking out my chin, I teased him, still trying for levity though I suspected he knew about the goblin visiting me at the falls. "And what do you see, then?"

"Your uncle hasn't left your side today, your aunt presented Sally with a week-long reservation for a cabin in Pigeon Forge, and I ran into that goblin and got a message to bring back to you."

Freddie had been missing all day, but I hadn't thought he might go hunting for trouble like that. "And just why on earth were you lookin' for her? If I'm supposed to fear her, why don't you?"

"Cause it ain't me she's after," Freddie said it before he could stop himself.

"Where did the two of you meet that she felt like she needed to send me a threat?" I hoped it wasn't in

Devil's Elbow. Not that I really feared the goblin, not deep down. I worried what she might do to those I loved more than anything she might do to me.

Freddie took a swig from his cup and looked around. I got the feeling he didn't want anyone else to overhear our conversation. "I was at the jailhouse in Cumberland Gap."

He paused for a moment. "More like I had just been to the jailhouse. I went to see Jessi and Arty. As you know, it ain't easy for people to lie to me. They always want to confess their deepest, darkest secrets and desires."

I didn't envy him that particular talent but I did wonder why he'd taken the time to see the only two people accused of murdering the goblin's husband. "And what did they have to say?"

Again, Freddie gave a mirthless laugh. "They blamed each other. Jessi told me that Roger had caught Arty cooking the books and Arty said that Jessi had called Roger's wife and told her of their affair. He says she wanted the woman to divorce Roger so she could have him."

He turned to fetch me some of what he was drinking, giving me time to chew on his news.

Somehow I wasn't surprised by any of it. I had wanted to think the best of Jessi, but the truth was, I didn't really know her. I only liked her because she'd saved Granny's magic show and seemed to have formed some small bond with me. As for Arty, I hadn't had time to get a handle on him. He was nowhere to be seen the night of the magic show or the next morning when Roger's body was found with Jessi standing over it, murder weapon in hand.

I accepted the red cup Freddie handed me and finally got out of my head and back to our conversation. "So the goblin was at the jailhouse too?"

"She may have been at some point, but I ran into her on my way back to Devil's Elbow. Right close to Cumberland Falls, to be exact. I braked hard to miss a deer that jumped across the road ahead of me and there she was, out of nowhere, standing in the middle of the road. We had a few words and then she just walked off into the woods."

I knew my face must have looked a sight to him as my expressions went from confusion to disbelief to careful amusement. "She can't be wrapped too tight to be hangin' around the woods like that. Is that normal goblin behavior?"

Freddie didn't find any of it funny. "There's no such thing as normal when it comes to goblins, Jo. You best remember that. Now, I can't stay here and not take Sally to Pigeon Forge because of Dixie's kindness, but I have a few elves watching over Devil's

Elbow. If it comes to it, they'll protect you and yours from the threat of the goblin."

Uncle Joe's voice wafted across the wide back yard of the bed and breakfast and I looked for Sally. Seeing her talking to Nadean Bodine and bouncing my friend's youngest on her hip, I nodded in Sally's direction. "Go dance with your lady, my friend. I'm awfully grateful for your help. I don't want you to think I'm not, but my family will do just fine. You've got to trust in us."

He kissed my cheek before leaving me to claim the hand of his lady for a dance. His parting words haunted me. "Oh but I do trust in your family, my dear. It's gonna take all of y'all, and my elves, to save the day."

Ray came and claimed my hand, leading me away to dance with him in the shadows just outside the light of the bonfire. He tipped my chin up and searched my eyes. "I'm hopin' that went better than it looked."

Sighing, I admitted there wasn't any good that had come from talking with Freddie. "He's worried about me, just like everyone else. I think y'all have forgotten I'm a pretty powerful witch in my own right."

"I don't see how anyone who knows you could ever forget that. Especially those of us who love you.

This business with the goblin is a real threat. You can't expect any of the witches, warlocks, or wolves in your family to just ignore that." Ray moved slow and easy with me in his arms and it was easy to relax against him.

Since Freddie and I had talked about more than the goblin, I shared what he told me about Jessi and Arty. "Seems like they're pointing fingers at each other, which shouldn't surprise me. They both had complicated relationships with Roger the magician. But I promised to help Jessi and now I'm not so sure that's the best thing to do."

Ray agreed. "I say tell your family lawyer of her plight, like you promised, and then step back. Judging by what the goblin told Freddie, that's best for everyone. Maybe if you stay away from the jailhouse, she'll stay away from you."

"I've thought about that all day. I know you're right, but it feels wrong to abandon Jessi. She ain't got a friend in the world. I'll call the lawyer tomorrow, but I'll have to think harder about leaving her to fend for herself."

Ray didn't argue and I was fairly certain that if I did just as he and Freddie wanted, the goblin would leave me alone. But where did that leave Jessie? And more importantly where did that leave Billy Jack and Genie? I'd called her on my lunch break to make sure she didn't need me to bring anything and she'd admitted that two of their opening weekend guests had cancelled their reservations.

The worry in her voice, that she tried to hide, broke me down. I wanted the bed and breakfast to soar and be a business she and Billy Jack would run for years and years to come. Not only because they were perfectly suited for it, but because it was the first time I'd ever known my cousin to stay on the right side of the law. There was a lot riding on the success of The Drunken Rooster. The pressure to play fairy godmother to two people I loved so much was almost unbearable. I hadn't forseen a murder upending the plans of my cousin and his beloved.

Ray felt the tension return to my body and to lighten the mood, he attempted to twirl me around. I say attempted because it ended with me on the ground in a fit of giggles and him apologizing profusely. "Jo, I'm so sorry baby. I thought I could do it since I was holding you just fine while we danced."

The poor ghost. I sat up and brushed pine needles from my clothes and hair. Walker Bodine came over and offered me a hand. I took it and stood, thanking him for his help. He leaned in close and I heard him sniffing the air as he brushed a stray needle from my shoulder.

I laughed and patted his arm. "It's okay, I'm not

drunk. Nowhere near it. Just clumsy, I guess."

His face turned beet red and he looked plumb mortified. "I'm sorry, Jo. It's just that you were over here alone dancin' around and Nadean was worried. Then when you went down like a sack of taters, well, I hopped right up to come help you. You wanna dance with me? Nadean won't mind, I promise."

My eyes welled up with tears but I dashed them away. I truly was blessed with friends and family who were always looking out for me. "I'd love that, Walker. I really would. Come on, let's cut a rug and show these young'uns how it's done."

Ray leaned in and kissed my cheek. "I don't mind neither, Jo."

Laughing, I left him in the shadows and followed Walker to the area by the bonfire where the music and dancing was in full swing.

Uncle Joe wasn't singing anymore. He was dancing with my friend Bonita and I watched them for a long minute admiring the way they fit together. Of a sudden, it didn't really matter to me that he was about a hundred years older than her. She was a grown witch who could choose her own romantic partner, and she was darned lucky if that happened to be my uncle. We could talk about it later, if she wanted. I didn't think it was anything that would change our friendship.

PJ and one of Walker's brothers, the youngest by the name of Ricky if I remembered right, who had come up from Tennessee for the wedding, were dancing near Bonita and Uncle Joe. I hadn't seen PJ since the wedding, but she looked happy as a clam.

I often envied how she could give her heart over and over in the eternal hope of finding the man of her dreams. Some called her names I won't repeat because of it, but I only ever saw the need to be loved and cherished shining in her eyes when she spoke of some new man she was seeing. Eternal optimism was her robe and a forgiving heart, her crown. Bless PJ, she was just like the rest of us, searching for our other half. Except in my eyes, she would always be the better half to whoever was out there waiting to be found by my redheaded, kindhearted best friend.

Walker and I waited until the Shifty River Boys struck up a song we could two-step to and we sure did cut a rug. It was the most fun I'd had in a long time. Don't get me wrong, being with Ray was fun, but it was a romantic kind of fun. Frolicking with friends was a different kind of fun that was the cure for what ailed me. I could worry about the weight of the world on my shoulders when the sun came up in the morning. Tonight I only wanted to dance with all the fellers and go home with the one that brought me when it was all said and done.

12

Dragging myself out of bed the next morning was the hardest thing I'd done in months. Being footloose and fancy free all over my mountains and down at the falls with Ray while Freddie ran the VV had spoiled me. If Delilah hadn't pounced on my chest, I would have hit my snooze button for the fourth time.

I gently shoved her off my chest and rolled out of bed, leaving her to burrow under my quilt and futilely chase Ray's ghostly form. Truth be told, she enjoyed this play time with him far more than she enjoyed waking me up. Ray provided both of us with endless distraction.

My face flamed as I recalled the sweet distraction last night when we got home from the barbecue. If it wasn't for that danged goblin, and the murder of the magician out at The Drunken Rooster, my life would be pretty close to perfect. As it stood, I had to bring my head out of the clouds and get back to the business of running my shop and my life while trying to figure out the trouble that had come to my cousin's door.

Snores from my living room reminded me that Uncle Joe had decided to bunk with me and I wondered just exactly when he'd let himself in for the night. Last I'd seen of him, he was standing with Bonita by her car out front of the bed and breakfast around two in the morning.

Pulling my robe tighter, I tiptoed into the kitchen and made myself some iced coffee, taking care to be quiet as a mouse. The aroma of coffee beans might wake Uncle Joe, but I took my tumbler of yummy iced vanilla caffeine goodness and sat in the window seat of my small dining room and looked out over town square. It was early yet, the sun was barely peeking over the horizon, and street lights were still on leaving shadows where their reach ended.

A movement from the corner of Main Street and Kentucky Avenue caught my eye, but my line of vision was blocked by a large sycamore tree. A sense of dread crawled up my spine and I thought about raising the window and leaning out so I could see who it was on the street below.

Delilah chose that moment to jump into my lap,

startling me. I squealed in surprise and spilled my coffee. Her disgruntled growl as she jumped back down and skittered under the dining room table caused me to forget the distraction outside my window.

"I'm so so sorry, girl," I crooned as I grabbed a roll of paper towels off the kitchen counter and mopped up the spilled coffee and ice. "Come on, let me feed you and then get myself ready for the day."

Uncle Joe's snores continued while I fixed up Delilah's breakfast. I was thankful we hadn't woken him with our fracas at the window. I knelt down beside my familiar as she ate and ran a hand firmly down her back. She looked up and mewled at me, her bright blue eyes full of love. I got her message loud and clear since I felt just the same. "You're going to be with me all day today, my dear. I've missed you too."

Leaving her, I padded to the bathroom and consoled myself with the promise of another iced coffee after I was ready to go down and open the VV. Ray was nowhere to be seen and so I hung up my robe and stripped down while turning the shower on full blast. I wanted hot, hot water and my best bar of honeysuckle, bergamot, and heart of clover soap. Reaching into the cabinet where I knew I had a bar stashed, I came up empty in my search. I opened the door wider and peered inside. Thinking I must be losing my mind, I searched every cabinet in the bathroom. No soap. Huh. I knew I had a bar because I'd made plenty before I left for my weeks alone in the woods. Granny, Aunt Dixie, and Genie had all been gifted a bar and I'd kept one for myself.

Shrugging, I sighed. I'd have to use my regular shower gel. Hopefully my day would go easier than it had started with creepy vibes at my front window, spilled coffee, and missing soap.

At noon, I looked up and breathed a sigh of relief that my shop was finally empty. It seemed everyone in Devil's Elbow had heard I was back at the VV. Sales had been brisk and I knew my friends and neighbors were truly happy to have me home where I belonged. Mrs. Parker, my old Sunday school teacher whose husband ran the feed store, pinched both my cheeks as I wrapped up four blown glass tumblers for her.

I'd given her a good discount and she'd winked at me as she declared I was her favorite student. "You know, between me and you, I always did like you best. You always knew all your bible verses and could rattle off the books of the Old Testament like a pro. Let's don't tell your cousin, hon. He has his own charms and a good teacher makes every child feel loved."

Laughing now at the memory of how she wanted me to keep her secret, I hurried to the front door and flipped the lock while making sure the *Gone to Lunch* sign was visible.

Before I could make it upstairs, PJ came through the beaded curtains from the back room. "Jo, wait up! I brought you lunch, hon!

Never one to turn down a free lunch, I made a twisting motion with my right hand and sent a spell out to lock the back door. "I reckon I am feelin' a bit peckish, Peej. What you got in that paper sack? Is it something from The Peapicking Panda?"

"Now how did you know that?" PJ stopped and balanced the sack on her hip, a pout forming on her bright red lips.

"Because my nose is working and, as my bestie for life, you know the way to my heart is food from the Panda! So turn that frown upside down and come on up buttercup, I ain't got more than an hour for lunch." I hurried upstairs knowing she'd follow on my heels.

Delilah and Uncle Joe were on the couch watching some court TV show and I shook my head at them. "Where's your pals? Don't tell me they're over at the bakery drivin' Aunt Dixie to distraction."

Uncle Joe ignored me but my familiar jumped down from his lap and licked her little chops as she lifted her nose and sniffed the air. I wasn't the only one who loved the food PJ had brought us.

"Oh no you don't, little miss," I scolded as she hopped up in the chair at the head of the table.

PJ shushed me and pulled a small container from the paper sack and opened it up. A strong fishy odor filled the room and Uncle Joe hopped up like his hind end was on fire and started opening windows. To say he didn't like the smell of this particular fish dish was putting it lightly. I laughed as my bestie placed the container on the chair beside Delilah.

"Dig in, sweetpea," PJ sang out to my sweet feline. "Missus Oskar said she caught them fresh this morning."

Rainbow trout was Delilah's favorite next to salmon. Since we had plenty of trout in the streams and lakes around Devil's Elbow, Missus Oskar, the owner of The Peapicking Panda restaurant, always made sure Delilah got a treat whenever any of us made an order.

She was a whole foot shorter than me, her hair still a raven black though she was older than Uncle Joe by a century, and the silk cheongsam dresses she wore were simply exquisite. Her magickal powers were the kind that made her successful in the restaurant business and I was grateful for them since I reaped the rewards of her delicious, magickal dishes.

Her family had come to these hills and hollers way back when her grandfather helped plan the railroads that carried coal and lumber from the region. Her maternal grandmother had met him back in San Francisco and our mountains had won her heart since her hometown in China had been in a mountainous region.

I thought I might take one of the blown glass fish that had come in with the tumblers over to Missus Oskar as a thank you. She would love the purple ones swirled with a pearlescent gold streak.

Waiting patiently for PJ to lift the boxes of fried rice and spring rolls, I poured sweet iced tea for us and took Uncle Joe a mason jar of lemonade.

"You want some food? Peej brought plenty." My plan was to lure my uncle away from the TV so we could grill him for the details of his relationship with Bonita. He didn't take the bait.

"I made myself a five egg omelette an hour ago while you were overrun with customers. I called one of those delivery services to bring you more eggs from the Pig." He swigged his lemonade, belched, and smiled at me.

"Alrighty then," I said, backing away slowly.

PJ had dished up our plates and I sat across from

her and bowed my head as she gave thanks for our meal. Uncle Joe made himself scarce as we began to eat. "I'm gonna head over to Dixie's for a little bit. You're in charge."

He didn't point at me or PJ when he delivered that order, but at Delilah. PJ giggled and I rolled my eyes. "Well duh, Uncle Joe, she's always in charge. Even when you're here."

"That's not what I meant short stack. She's in charge of guarding you while I'm gone. Be sure to take her down with you when you open the shop again." He waved goodbye to PJ and took off before I could defend my ability to watch out for my own self.

"Who put a bee in his bonnet?" PJ asked as she lifted her tea for a sip.

Sighing, I thought about how much I needed to tell her. Thinking it might be good for PJ to know, and realizing in that moment that Uncle Joe had likely warned Bonita since they seemed to be an item, I caved. "There's a mad goblin on the loose and apparently she's got her eye set on me."

"Okaaaaay," my friend said, her eyes narrowing. "But why you and what brought her to Devil's Elbow anyway?"

"She was married to the magician who was murdered at The Drunken Rooster." I kept it short and simple. Telling PJ everything that had happened since the murder would take longer than my lunch hour.

"Wait, I thought that girl Jessi was his girlfriend. He sure didn't act like he was a married man that night. He flirted with anyone in a skirt the entire time. I felt really bad for Jessi cause she's way too cute to put up with that."

I nodded and speared some orange chicken with my fork. "Well, she's sittin' in the jailhouse over in the Gap right now on suspicion of murder. Hadn't you heard?"

PJ's face fell. "I surely didn't know that, and that's real odd since my clients are the best gossips."

"Well, they wouldn't have known who Jessi was if they weren't at the weddin'. And even if they were, the next morning was utter chaos. Most folks saw the police out in force and just wanted to get back to Devil's Elbow without askin' too many questions," I reasoned with myself as well as with PJ.

Lots of our friends and neighbors had been at the wedding and plenty had pitched tents out back so as not to drive the twisty, winding roads back to Devil's Elbow in the dark while being three sheets to the wind from the wedding supper. And no one ever wanted to have trouble with the law, so they had skedaddled that morning instead of lingering to pick up what gossip there was to overhear.

"Well," my sweet friend opined, "I sure hope that gal has someone to help her in her time of trouble. How are Genie and Billy Jack doin'? I can't imagine having a murder at my salon a week before the grand opening."

"And now you see my problem. I was hopin' to figure out who did it, but the goblin has been hounding me and people connected to me. I may have found a relic she wanted and allowed Freddie to send it to the Seelie Court."

"Oh, that's not good. That's really bad, Jo. You better listen to your uncle. I'm gonna call Bonita too and see if we can't bolster his magic with our own. Every little bit will be a help if that goblin comes after you." PJ picked up her phone to call Bonita and there was no talking her down.

Looking over at Delilah, who'd finished her fish and was now mewling at me for something off my plate, I shook my head and placed my dish on the floor. "My appetite is gone, sweet girl. You can have whatever you like."

 ⓭

Before PJ left, she complained that her favorite slippers, the ones I'd given her for her birthday, were missing from the back room of her salon. Since I had an extra pair just like them still in stock, I handed them over on the house.

She hugged me tight and kissed my cheek while Delilah stretched out in the front window, luxuriating in the sun. "Oh, thank you so much Jo! After wearing these heels all day," she looked down at her bright orange six-inch stilettos, "I need my slippers at closin' time. I'd never get the shop cleaned up and sorted for the next day without them. You're a real doll, you know that?"

"Well at least you think so," I teased as I walked with her to the back door. "But you best scoot on down the alley and get ready for your afternoon clients."

She hurried through the door as I held it open and disappeared quick as a flash. Turning, I made my way back to the front.

Delilah mewled her orders to me from the window without moving a muscle to get up and I huffed out a breath at being bossed around by my familiar. But I gave in to her demand anyway and made the motion to lock the back door of the VV again like I had after PJ had come through it earlier.

Anger rose in my chest at having to change my routine. I wasn't accustomed to living in fear. Especially in my own home. Another meowed message from Delilah set me straight. "I know, I know. It isn't fear so much as being smarter about looking out for the both of us. I know that lock wouldn't stop the goblin, but it might keep her from gettin' the drop on us."

Satisfied that she'd got through to me, Delilah went back to twitching her tail as she settled down for a snooze after her too large meal at lunch.

Moving around the shop, I passed the hours cleaning and restocking the items that weren't one of a kind or vintage. The hours passed in a blur and since no one else came in, I didn't realize it was closing time until Aunt Dixie came by, the only person to disturb the bell over the door since lunch.

"What happened to you, child?" she asked, looking me up and down. "Looks like you been diggin' in the coal mines instead of keepin' shop."

I brushed a strand of hair back and looked down at my clothes. I was dusty and a few cobwebs I'd dusted from the corners stuck here and there on the lace trim along the hem of my tank top. I gave a half-hearted grin as I tried to fix my appearance. "Now, Aunt Dixie, it's not as bad as all that."

She leaned in and rubbed a smudge of dirt off my cheek with a wet thumb. I almost cringed but knew any sass on my part would only send her mother hen instincts into overdrive. Instead, I mumbled my thanks and skipped away from her to look into the mirror and fix my own face.

"Lordy, I tell you what, I'm so glad today is done. Them Shifty River Boys and your uncle are more than I can handle right now. I put up with them because Clint, the bass player, can bake almost better'n me. But don't you tell him that. His help is worth all the aggravation. I've gone and misplaced my best rolling pin in all the fracas. I wondered if you might help me find it." My aunt busied herself rearranging all the bobby pins that held up her messy bun.

"I'd be happy to help. Come to think of it, I'm missin' a bar of that honeysuckle soap I made before I went off on my campin' trip. And PJ is missin' the slippers I gave her for her birthday. Coincidence, you think?" I leaned closer to the mirror to inspect my face. All clean. I didn't need to change before going to help Aunt Dixie.

Delilah wanted to go back upstairs and so I took a moment to let her back into the apartment. I called out for Ray but there was no answer. For a moment, I wondered where he'd been all day. It wasn't unusual for him to stay gone now that his mother could see him, but he usually gave me a goodbye kiss and a head's up before he left.

Promising Delilah I'd be back in time for dinner, I closed the door and hurried downstairs to go with Aunt Dixie. It was a warm evening and I was happy to get outside again and feel a breeze sweep my skirt against my legs.

"I declare, it was so good to be up in my mountains alone for two weeks. I wish I could go back." My voice was wistful as I looked up at the evergreen forest that surrounded Devil's Elbow.

Aunt Dixie snorted. "Honey, wouldn't we all like to just wander the woods when we felt like it? But ain't none of us got a money tree, not even us witches. Besides, everyday ain't as busy for you as today was. You'll be back in the swing of things before you know it."

She was right. I had been thrilled to see all our friends and neighbors and to spend the day with Delilah. My familiar had come to see me once or twice during my camping trip but she did love her creature comforts, as they were.

"Freddie and Sally did real well keeping the VV up and runnin'. I hope it gave him the desire to open his own business here in town." It was a secret wish I'd had for the pair and spoken aloud, it seemed entirely possible.

"Oh, I think Sally bein' here is all that's needed to persuade him. He would do well in business, what with his natural elf charm and good looks. What kind of shop do you think he'd like? I mean, he was really good at managing folks during the baking competition," Aunt Dixie mused as I held the door for her.

We went inside and I paused as she turned the latch on the front door to its locked position. "I bet he could run a really nice breakfast shop with Sally's help. Like a to-go place so they only have to worry about hirin' a few employees and have the afternoons to themselves."

Aunt Dixie's eyes brightened. "You know, that ain't such a bad idea if I do say so myself! I've been wantin' to open later in the mornin', but worried about the breakfast crowd. They've got used to my biscuits, you know."

I didn't know my aunt wasn't up to the early morning hours any longer. "Well now, don't go puttin' the cart before the horse, so to speak. We don't know that Freddie even wants to stay here. I guess it all depends on Sally, as you said. If you need help in the mornings, I could come down and lend a hand."

Aunt Dixie snorted again as we headed into the kitchen. "Ain't no need with these fellers stayin' upstairs!"

She shoo'd them all away except for Clint. Speaking with urgency, she set us to work. "Alrighty you two, let's find my rollin' pin before they get the idea they'd like supper here too."

My aunt's cell phone rang half way through our shake down of the back end of the bakery and she bustled up front to let Billy Jack and Genie inside. I was happier than a pig in mud to see them. Digging around for that rolling pin was not as fun as you'd think.

"Hey, you two! What brings you into town this evenin'?" I called out and went up front with them to keep Aunt Dixie from returning to the kitchen. Clint was on his own. Hopefully, he was smart enough to beat feet while my aunt's back was turned.

Genie pulled me aside as Aunt Dixie poured some

iced tea for us. She shoved a brown, manila envelope into my hands. "I found these papers in Arty's room when I was in there cleaning up this afternoon. I guess the police missed them."

Taking the envelope, I stared at Genie. My amazement must have shown plainly on my face. She patted my arm and smiled like a cat who got the cream. "Just because I'm not magickal like the rest of you doesn't mean I don't have a few tricks up my sleeve."

Shaking my head, I assured her I wasn't in doubt where her smarts were concerned. "Honey child, if there's one thing I know about you it's that you're sharp as a tack. What surprises me is that the police missed this envelope in Arty's room."

Genie shrugged. "He hid it pretty well and they were undermanned at the time. Unless someone was looking for it specifically, or accustomed to cleaning thoroughly, they would have missed it. The old vanity mama gave me to help furnish The Drunken Rooster was mine growin' up. I knew it inside and out. Arty found the false bottom in the drawer where I hid my diary. He used it to hide that envelope."

"Well then, there must be something awfully bad in here," I said as I unwound the red string that kept the flap of the envelope secure.

Genie's eyes lit up. "Oh and how! He's listed the

fees he negotiated with each place Roger and Jessi performed. Since the one he listed for The Drunken Rooster is substantially less than what we paid, I'd say old Arty was cookin' the books for some time."

As I pulled out the two papers in the envelope, I saw the list Genie mentioned. Even though I knew next to nothing about how much a business manager might charge for a show, the numbers looked awfully low to me. A thought occurred as I went over the list. "It'd be easy as pie to call each place and see what they paid, but I bet Uncle Joe might be able to tell us if any of these numbers sound right."

Confusion replaced the excitement in Genie's eyes at my musings. "How would Uncle Joe know anything about it?"

"The Shifty River Boys, of course! They play gigs here and there all around the state. I bet they pull in a performance fee akin to what a magic show would." Sometimes I surprised myself but Genie wasn't the least bit doubtful of my mental prowess.

"See? That's why I brought this straight to you! I knew you'd know just what to do. So do you think Arty killed Roger to cover up his embezzlement?" Genie spoke out loud exactly what I'd been thinkin' since Jessi told me Arty was the last person she saw with Roger.

"I don't know, but if I was a bettin' woman, I'd bet the farm on it."

Genie's face fairly glowed with satisfaction. "You go on home and sit down with Uncle Joe, then. We'll wait here till y'all come back and then all go out for dinner and figure out the next step."

I hugged Ray's sister tight and then rushed out the front door of the bakery as she explained everything to Aunt Dixie, who was fussin' at my retreating back to beat the band about her missing rolling pin.

⬤14

By the time Uncle Joe confirmed my suspicions about Arty's doctored figures, it was too late to get a good seat at any of the restaurants we liked and so we all just headed over to Aunt Dixie's house for dinner.

I was in the midst of making a good garden salad from veggies Aunt Dixie had picked from Granny's garden when I thought of Ray. "Hey y'all, has anyone seen my boyfriend today? He might be over at his mama's house, but he usually checks in with me at some point in the day. I can't see him goin' all day without checkin' on me with this goblin on the loose."

Genie stopped stirring the pitcher of sweet tea on the counter and cocked her head. "I just talked to mama on the way over here and she said she hasn't seen him all day. He was supposed to come by this mornin' and sit with her for awhile in her flower shop."

Worry bloomed in my chest and I tried to fight it down. "Maybe he's been ridin' shotgun with Deputy Carter? I know he likes to indulge his lawman side now and again."

Uncle Joe nodded in agreement as he took the stack of plates Aunt Dixie handed him. "I bet that's it short stack. He'll be back at the VV waitin' on us when we get home, no doubt."

As much as I wanted to believe Ray was just off doing his own thing, I couldn't completely dismiss my concerns. Until that goblin was out of our neck of the woods, I knew I wouldn't rest easy.

Placing the salad bowl on the table alongside the other dishes Aunt Dixie had whipped up, I sat with my family and bowed my head as Uncle Joe said grace. His long-winded prayer made me feel like a kid again, making my growling stomach wait and willing my eyes to remain closed even though the delicious scents of dinner tempted me.

Soon enough, all the bowls and platters were passed around and we got down to the business of eating. Billy Jack filled us in on the small improvements he was making to the brewery while they waited for the grand opening. Uncle Joe said he would have another truck of plums brought from Flat

Lick to make certain my cousin had enough for the brandy he was planning to have ready after summer was past.

"Jo, I meant to tell you earlier that we had two new reservations almost as soon as those others cancelled! I forgot in all the excitement over Arty's papers." Genie smiled with satisfaction and I was deeply grateful for her new bookings.

Aunt Dixie caught onto the other info she mentioned. "Who on earth is Arty?"

Uncle Joe wiped his mouth and dropped his napkin on his empty plate. "He's the business manager for that magician. They've got him in the pokey over at Cumberland Gap as a murder suspect. It seems Genie found some incriminating evidence at the bed and breakfast today."

"Well then, our problems should be solved, right?" My aunt was pleased with the news about Arty but I knew it wouldn't be so easy to get rid of the goblin who wanted the pendant Freddie had sent to the Seelie queen.

"I wish it was that easy, Aunt Dixie. But, as usual, I seem to have brought my troubles on myself. There was something else the police missed at the bed and breakfast. And that's the real reason the goblin has me in her sights." I blew out a breath of relief that I'd finally shared the truth with my entire family.

Uncle Joe stood and crossed his arms, his gaze honing in on my face. "It's that relic Freddie sent to the Seelie Court isn't it? I wish you'd have come to me first, short stack."

I stood and threw my own napkin down on the table. "It's not that easy, Uncle Joe. The goblin came into the VV with Arty and somehow she made that relic move from my pocket to a spot in the glass case of my counter. Freddie worked his own magick to snatch it out from under her. He saved my bacon. I'm not second guessing him and nothing was done to purposely keep you in the dark."

Aunt Dixie shook her head and stood to clear the table. "You should have told us about finding that relic at the bed and breakfast, Jolene. My son should have known so he could better protect Genie and his business."

Although I knew my aunt was right, I hadn't meant to hamstring my cousin. "I didn't know who it belonged to when I found it or even what it really was I had. I thought it was only something that belonged to the killer because it gave me the sight when I touched it."

The clanking of plates, glasses and silverware ceased as my family, to a one, looked at me in confusion.

Billy Jack's voice broke the silence. "So you know who the killer is? Why haven't you said?"

"Of course I don't know! I only saw a flash of what happened as if I was in the killer's shoes. If I knew who had killed Roger, I surely would have told the police by now. Do you think I want your business to suffer? Do you think I want a goblin huntin' me down?"

I fought back tears of frustration as I turned away from them. Uncle Joe came to my side and led me out of the dining room and onto the front porch where I could let my tears fall without an audience.

"Look here short stack, no one in there thinks for a minute that you would put any of us in harm's way. It's just that sometimes you try so hard to handle everything yourself in the mistaken belief that the rest of us need protection. We're all capable of holding our own against a goblin." His words struck a nerve but I didn't let him off the hook either.

"Isn't that what you're doing to me? You should be with Bonita, makin' sure she's safe instead of sleeping on my couch."

My uncle didn't take kindly to my interference in this personal life. "What happens between me and Bonita is my business, niece. And I don't kiss and tell so sleepin' on her couch isn't something you'd even know about. You're making assumptions and you know what that does."

Chastised, and rightly so, by his words, I swiped at my eyes and threw up my hands. "You're right and I'm wrong. I have no idea what I'm doing or saying. I've never seen anything like this goblin and being the mouse to her cat has my nerves on edge. I'm worried sick about Ray right now, something's not right with him and I can feel it. Uncle Joe, I need you to do more than sleep on my couch!"

I hated having what amounted to a temper tantrum on my uncle but the events of the past few days had finally broken me. Instead of keeping his distance, my sweet, gruff uncle pulled me into his arms and basically patted my head.

"Now now, short stack. I'm not mad at you and I'm not blaming you for any of this mess. Come on, let's go find Deputy Carter and give him that envelope Genie found. He can take it over to Cumberland Gap tomorrow. Then we'll go back to the VV and if Ray ain't there, I'll help you find him."

I hugged my uncle around the neck and murmured my thanks. "And don't tell anyone else about my temper tantrum, okay?"

"My lips are sealed, short stack. I'll go in and tell Dixie where we're goin' so she doesn't worry. You wait right here, promise?"

"Cross my heart," I said as I made an x over that part of my anatomy. I watched him go inside and then turned to look out over Aunt Dixie's huge front yard. The moon was bright and I could see it from where I stood. I wished on a shooting star that streaked across the darkened sky. "I hope you're okay wherever you are Ray Danged Davis."

Deputy Carter stood outside his police cruiser on Main Street waiting on us to pull up beside him. I'd called him as my uncle drove us back into town and told him about Genie's discovery and our theory that Arty was cooking the books. He agreed that it was evidence the police over in the Gap needed to have ASAP.

Uncle Joe swung his big blue truck into the spot beside the deputy's cruiser and hopped out with the envelope in hand. "Here you go, son. If Sheriff Quinn takes issue with how you received this information, feel free to give him my name. His own cousin missed it in the sweep of the bed and breakfast, so they ought to be grateful for my family turnin' it in."

"The sheriff is out of town at the moment, so he won't be a problem. I'll take this over tonight since it's evidence in a murder investigation. I expect Arty the business manager will be charged in the next 24 hours, at least." Deputy Carter leaned into the open driver's side window of his car and dropped the envelope inside. When he faced us again, he held out a hand to Uncle Joe. "Thanks for bringing this to me, Joe."

Before we parted ways, I took hold of the deputy's arm. "Have you seen Ray today? I know he likes to ride patrol with you from time to time."

My voice was hopeful and Deputy Carter picked up on it. "I sure haven't, Jolene. Is he missin' or something?"

I tried to keep my face from showing the mounting worry that clawed at me. "Well, we can't exactly file a missing person's report can we? There's no such thing as a missing ghost report."

"Maybe he's out at his mama's house?" Deputy Carter's question was hopeful and his expression revealed that he was concerned for us.

Uncle Joe shook his head. "Genie called her earlier. Mrs. Davis hasn't seen him today."

"I'll surely keep an eye out for him on my patrols. Y'all let me know if he doesn't turn up by tomorrow, you hear?"

I shook my head in agreement as I didn't trust myself to speak without sounding whiny. Deputy Carter didn't press me and I appreciated that. He shook my uncle's hand again and then took off for Cumberland Gap with the evidence we'd given him.

Uncle Joe and I turned toward the VV. There weren't any lights on, not even upstairs and I could see the glow of Delilah's eyes in the front window of my apartment. Happy that at least she was safe and sound, I took the hand my uncle offered and crossed the street.

Not only was Ray still missing, but when I opened the door to our apartment, Delilah was transformed into her full painter and she was jumpy as a horned toad on a hot rock. Uncle Joe took hold of my arm before I could even get my apartment door shut. "Something's not right, Jolene. My wolf can smell that our goblin friend has been here and not so long ago either."

Kneeling, I pulled Delilah close to me. If that goblin was in our home, I wanted to protect my familiar. "But how would she break the wards on this place, Uncle Joe?"

I didn't understand goblins, or even know how powerful their magick could be, but I knew Freddie's magick also protected the VV on top of my own.

My uncle placed a finger to his lips and moved

with the grace of his wolf towards my bedroom. The door was closed and I couldn't remember if I'd closed it earlier in the day. It wasn't my way to do such a thing since I wanted Delilah to have the full run of the place when I was gone. My heart leapt into my throat when he threw open the door and dashed inside.

Delilah growled and used the full weight of her mountain lion form to keep me from following Uncle Joe. In a moment, he was back in the doorway beckoning me to his side. "Come have a look, short stack. Something tells me that goblin got what she came for and left as soon as she heard us comin' up the stairs."

Hurrying to his side, I pulled up short at the sight of my room. It was turned upside. The quilt and pillows from my bed were on the floor and the mattress was shredded to pieces. Bottles from the top of my vanity were smashed in the floor, their green, pink, and blue shards glittering from the moonlight that streamed in through the broken window frame.

At once, as I crossed the room to the open jewelry box still sitting atop the mahogany dresser Granny had given me when I moved into my apartment, I knew what the creature had taken. My summoning stone. Reaching for the empty burgundy velvet pouch where I'd kept it since returning from the mountains, my heart sank at the proof it was gone.

I couldn't think straight, but Uncle Joe sure could. "Well now all the missin' things around town make sense. That goblin is gatherin' up talismans to set against you, against all of us. If this ain't a fine kettle of fish."

Feeling the world spin around me, I thought of Ray. Uncle Joe came to my side, as did Delilah. The two of them kept me on my feet as I called out my boyfriend's name knowing there would be no answer. I broke free from their hold to dart around my empty apartment, desperation driving me on a mission I knew would be fruitless. Everywhere I looked, every call of his name, brought nothing but more pain and regret.

"How? How did she take Ray from me? He's a ghost. A spirit."

Uncle Joe led me to a seat at my small dining room table, his expression full of sorrow for the madness he surely saw in my eyes and heard in my voice. "Jolene, does it really matter at this point? Odds are she has Ray, but like you said, he's a spirit and not a living bein' she can harm. If anything, she's planning to use him as bait to catch you and get her relic back."

Misery settled in bones. "But I don't have it! Can't she see it's not here?"

"But you can make Freddie bring it back for her. I'm sure if Sally was in town, she'd probably have taken her instead. But since you're close to him, and under the protection of his elves, you're the next best thing. And I'd like to know what kind of protection they are to let this happen on their watch." Uncle Joe said the last part loudly as though the walls had ears.

To my great surprise, two elves that had been best men at Granny's wedding to Mr. B appeared before us. They were not the least bit pleased by Uncle Joe's complaint against them.

"Miss Jolene," the one who'd danced with PJ at the wedding addressed me while studiously ignoring my uncle. "The goblin has not been in Devil's Elbow tonight. Your stone was taken by the ghost who holds your heart and soul. He was compelled by the goblin's power. There was nothing we could do to help him and all he wanted was to get away before you came home."

I felt my heart breaking into a million pieces to know that Ray was being used against me. Standing, I thanked the elves for their help. "Please don't take offense, my uncle didn't mean anything by what he said. It's just that we never expected any of this."

The other elf glanced warily at Uncle Joe. "No

offense taken, Miss Jolene. I wish there was more we could have done for your boyfriend, but I have a feeling he can hold his own with the goblin because of his incorporeal nature. Goblins can't harm ghosts."

With that, the two elves turned to leave and Uncle Joe got up to walk out with them. The words the elf had shared about Ray being safe from the goblin lit a fire under my behind and I rushed to my room to put everything right again. This was my home with Ray and Delilah and I'd be darned if some goblin was going to rattle me. I owed it to the ones I loved to come out fighting.

With a few simple spells, I had the broken window fixed, my bed repaired as good as new, and the broken glass bottles rejoined and returned to their place on my vanity. I knew I wouldn't sleep a wink, but at least I'd reclaimed some peace in my home.

When Uncle Joe returned, he popped popcorn while I switched on the TV. Delilah slowly let go of her painter form and jumped up in my lap for a marathon snuggle session. After two mysteries and a comedy special, Uncle Joe had nodded off, his soft snores comforting me. Delilah's purrs of contentment lulled me and her small, warm body was better than any afghan. With their drowsy company, I fell asleep sometime before dawn.

The next morning as I stood behind the cash register of the VV, Jessi the magician's assistant waltzed right through the front door like a bird flown from its prison cage. I noticed the small piece of luggage she'd left by the front door.

"Jolene!" she cried out and made a beeline for me, throwing her arms out and hugging me across the expanse of counter between us.

I hardly knew what to say, but it wasn't really all that surprising to see her since Deputy Carter had gone out to the Gap the night before to turn over the incriminating papers Genie had found. "I take it you're a free woman now."

The words sounded as lame to my ears as they likely did to hers. But if they did, she sure didn't let on. Jessi finally let me go and stood back. Her smile lit up the room. "I am and it feels amazing! That young, handsome deputy friend of yours said it was all on account of your cousin's girlfriend. Said she found the papers that cooked Arty's goose. Since I didn't want to go back there, because of the murder and all, I came here to thank you instead."

It was good to see her, I had to admit. "I'm just happy they got the killer. It's shocking that someone so close to Roger ended up being the one that did him in."

As soon as the words were out of my mouth, I recalled that Ray had told me that was the usual way of things when it came to crimes of passion. Greed, lust, and envy sure did cause a whole passel of pain. As did the absence of my boyfriend.

Jessi's smile faltered as she nodded in agreement. "I would never in a million years have thought Arty capable of such a thing, but I didn't think he'd steal from Roger either. Just goes to show, you never really know some people."

"Ain't that the truth," a voice behind me piped up and I turned to find Freddie and Sally walking in from the back room.

As happy as I was to see them, they had come home too soon. Poking my finger in Freddie's chest, I chastised him. "I thought y'all was gonna stay longer in Pigeon Forge than that!"

Sally spoke up to defend her man. "Believe me, Jo, he wanted to stay once we got there but I was itchin' to be back home. I kept having this feelin' like something wasn't right."

"Well, everything is set to rights now and it's so good to see y'all again," Jessi said and reached her hand across the counter to shake hands with my friends.

Freddie smiled, but I noticed it was lacking his usual easy charm. He seemed to be sizing Jessi up. "They must've decided someone else murdered the magician, then?"

"Jolene and I were just sayin' how surreal it was that Arty killed Roger." Jessi looked at me and I nodded.

"Genie found some papers in his room at the bed and breakfast that showed how he was embezzling funds from Roger. I guess the magician found out that night and they argued. Jessi heard the beginning of it but didn't know how it would end."

Freddie cocked his head to the side and looked at Jessi again. "So you heard them arguing?"

"Yeah, it wasn't unusual for them to have words, so I went back upstairs. So many times since, I've wished I hadn't left Roger alone with him." Jessi's voice cracked with emotion and I came around the counter to comfort her.

Even if she had turned out to be the other woman in Roger's life, she'd lost someone she loved to a violent death and been the one to discover his body. Giving my elf friend the side eye as I turned Jessi toward the front door, I admonished my friend. "That's enough for now. She ain't been out of jail all of two minutes."

Freddie shrugged and took Sally's hand. "Well, since you've got things in hand here, we're gonna go on down and see Dixie. Later, I'd like to talk business with you, Jolene."

At once, I wished Jessi wasn't with us. I hoped the business Freddie wanted to discuss was about him opening a shop in town.

When my friends were gone, Jessi gave me another hug. "I'm just so grateful for your family Jolene! I don't know what I would've done without y'all. Seems like everybody around here feels the same."

Heat rushed to my face and I mumbled a denial. My family never did a thing so that folks were reliant upon us. We did good to our neighbors because they'd always done right by us. "Devil's Elbow is a special place. Everybody here is an important part of our town."

Jessi frowned, her eyes showing her sadness. "I

wish I had a hometown. I haven't lived in one place since I left home at sixteen."

My heart ached for the young woman standing before me. She didn't look much older than a high school senior and suddenly, I wondered how old she really was. "Are you sayin' you ain't got any family you can go back to? No cousins, even? You don't look a day older than nineteen."

She rocked back on her heels, her hands going to her back pockets. "I turned twenty-one yesterday. And no, I sure don't have kinfolk to take me in. If my aunt or uncle saw me again, they'd slam the door in my face. So, I'm basically on my own now."

My mouth hung open as I took hold of her shoulder. "You mean to tell me you spent your birthday as a jailbird? That ain't right! You've got to stay here at least long enough for us to throw you a party. All I have is a sofa bed upstairs, but you're welcome to it for as long as you'd like to stay."

I could tell there hadn't been many people in Jessi's life who had offered her much kindness. She stammered her words, but I understood she was overwhelmed by the offer. "Oh, wow, Jolene. I hadn't...I meant I didnt'...Oh, I don't know what to say."

"Say you'll stay for just a little while and I'll take

care of the rest. And since it was your birthday yester-day, you can have your pick from any of the dresses you like in my shop. They're all vintage, and you'd be so pretty in any of them. Choose a party dress cause we're gonna have a hoedown in your honor!" Laughing, I steered her toward the rack of dresses that occupied a space in the back corner of the shop.

Jessi swiped the tears from her eyes and did as I asked without another word. Delilah came down and I picked her up, eager to introduce her to our new houseguest.

"Oh, my!" Jessi exclaimed when she saw my familiar, "I'm terribly allergic to cats. Is she yours?"

Delilah squirmed out of my arms and landed on the floor between me and Jessi. She looked up at our guest and cocked her head, seemingly puzzled by my new friend. "Oh, that's not good! I'm so sorry. I had no idea. Come on Delilah, back upstairs you go."

Jessi sneezed three times as I lifted my sweet kitty and carried her up and left her there with my regrets. "It's only until I find someplace else for her to stay, my sweet."

Delilah mewled her disapproval but I couldn't have her running loose with Jessi downstairs. As I hurried back down, I thought of where else my friend could stay.

There were three other spaces just like my shop,

that my parents had left to me, which were currently empty. Any one of the apartments above them would be suitable for Jessi if she chose to stay for a while.

She stood holding the gorgeous blue silk dress that had come in the week before. I'd hardly had time to lay eyes on it, but I knew it was one I'd wanted to keep for myself. Instead of entertaining a moment of regret, I wished her a happy birthday and went to retrieve the keys to one of the empty storefronts. "Let's get you set up in an apartment that won't leave you sneezing."

Jessi took the handkerchief I handed her and tended her poor, reddened nose. "I don't know how I got so lucky as to meet you when I did, Jolene. You're a lifesaver!"

She took hold of the handle of her rolling suitcase and followed me out the front door of the VV. In minutes, we'd crossed town square and gone through the front door of a shop that used to be a circulating library of sorts. There were still stacks of paperbacks sitting around, and some hardback books here and there, and Jessi grew excited by the possibilities. "Oh, I do love to read! This place is like heaven. It's such a shame it's closed."

"Well, the elderly woman who ran it passed on last year and there was no one else to take on the project. I've thought about hiring someone to re-open it and try to make it profitable myself, but it seems like I've been busy with so many other things that I never have the time to devote to it." I thought of having someone come in and at least give all the shelves a good dusting.

As we gained the stairs to the apartment above, I flipped on the lightswitch that illuminated the way and went ahead of Jessi. "Now, this apartment isn't as large as mine. As a matter of fact, it's like a one-room situation with a murphy bed and a kitchenette, but it's clean, the furniture is gently used, and I can send you over some toiletries and fresh towels."

Jessi lifted her suitcase and came quickly up behind me. "I have some things from traveling around so much. Souvenirs as they say, my own make-up bag, clothes, and some body wash and shampoo. I'm sure whatever's in there will work for my meager needs."

"Alrighty then, I guess you can settle in without me hanging around, but I'd love it if you joined us all for supper. We'll probably go to Kudzu's after Aunt Dixie closes the bakery. Just be back over at the VV by half past five if you'd like to come with, okay?"

Jessi placed her suitcase on the small sofa and turned to look around the room. "I just might take you up on that. Food at the jail wasn't all that great. And this place will do just fine. Thank you again,

Jolene. I really can't thank you enough for all you've done. You must be an angel."

"Oh hardly! Believe me. But my granny always said to do unto others as you'd have them do unto you. I guess it sunk in. Besides, you saved the day for us at Granny's wedding and that gets you bonus points in our family. If you make her happy, you make all of us happy."

Jessi's laughter filled the small one-room apartment and she took my hand. "I'll try and remember that."

I gave her the keys and said my goodbyes so she could have some time to herself to freshen up or take a nap, or just get her bearings in a new place. I was pleased she was as fond of books as I was and wondered if down the road, she might like to re-open the circulating library.

Shaking my head, I crossed the street and headed back to my own shop. It was becoming the norm for me to want to set up all my friends and family in business to keep them near.

Later in the afternoon, Freddie and Sally came back as I was opening a few new boxes of inventory by the front window. The sunlight streaming through had called to me and sitting cross legged on the floor in a puddle of sunshine and popping the bubble wrap from the boxes hardly seemed like work.

I stood when they came in and Sally laughed as she picked up a stray piece of the bubble wrap. "Don't get up for us, Jo. We'll sit with you and help unpack the boxes."

Freddie agreed. "This spot is the best one in the whole shop. That's why Delilah always holds court there on the window ledge."

My familiar mewled at Freddie and we all laughed. Sitting down again with my friends, I let them each take a box. "I'm glad you two came back. I wanted to tell you I could go stay with Genie and Billy Jack and let y'all have my apartment again."

Sally unwrapped one of the handmade wooden dolls I'd ordered from a lady over in Gatlinburg. "We couldn't do that! You're home and besides, we can stay with Red."

I looked at Sally's face watching her expression to see if the idea of staying with her brother bothered her.

Freddie took hold of my hand. "They are kin, Jolene, and Sally grew up there. It's home no matter the troubles that are past. And they've been workin' on their relationship. Red has to go out of town for work this week so we won't be underfoot. Truth be told, he was happy we could come and house sit for him."

Relief flooded me and I smiled at Sally. "I'm

happy to hear it. I've been worried about y'all and that's all I'm gonna say on it."

"And that's enough," she said and smiled back, her eyes dancing with joy.

"Now," Freddie said, his voice growing serious, "we need to talk about what an elf needs to do to set up shop here in Devil's Elbow. I hear you're the land-lady for most of the empty shops around here."

I laughed and put down the small satin pillow I'd unwrapped from my box. "A little bird must have told you about me and Aunt Dixie hopin' you would put down roots here."

Dinner at Kudzu's was chicken fried steak, mashed taters, and brown gravy. Merlene, the owner of the cafe, had her famous banana pudding on the menu and Aunt Dixie sniffed at the selection when our waitress came to inquire about coffee and dessert. "I reckon I'll just have coffee, thank you."

I had to try hard to hold back my laughter until the waitress had finished our dessert order and left the table. "Aunt Dixie, it wouldn't kill you to try Merlene's signature puddin'. It ain't often she puts on an apron anymore."

"And thank the Lord for that! She ought to go on and let her son have her recipe, it ain't like it's anything special anway. Most everybody and their mother can make banana puddin', it's easier than fallin' off a log. That's why I can't understand how she messes it up so bad." Aunt Dixie fussed and carried on about it until Uncle Joe told her to pipe down.

"Dixie you'd talk the birds outta the trees! Settle down now and let's hear what my niece has planned for Miss Jessi's birthday celebration."

At the mention of her name, my new friend tried to get on my aunt's good side. "I'd love to hear how Dixie makes banana puddin'. I love it, but I have no idea how it's made."

Billy Jack looked at Jessi like she had two heads. "What kinda southern woman don't know how to make some good banana puddin'?"

Uncle Joe was sitting beside him and promptly hushed him up. "Boy, act like you got some manners and apologize to Miss Jessi. She ain't even a married woman yet. Everybody has to learn things in their own time."

Genie's cheeks flamed a bright red and she placed a hand on Billy Jack's as she turned to Jessi. "Please forgive this big old heathen of mine, Jessi. My mama taught me to make it when I was little but I didn't try my hand at it until recently. It's really not too difficult. I can show you if you'd like."

Aunt Dixie chimed in as the waitress arrived with coffee and our desserts. "If anyone's gonna teach her, it'll be me. That way, there'll be one more woman who knows how to make a good banana puddin' in the world."

Jessi seemed excited to be the center of attention at our big table. "I'd love to learn from the both of you. I was raised by an aunt and uncle. At least that's how I was told to address them growing up. They adopted me but never wanted to be known as my mother and father."

Her face and voice as she told us this sad news was free of care or worry. It seemed like she'd accepted long ago that her adoptive family behaved like any normal aunt or uncle would. I had my doubts since she'd told me at the VV that they basically wanted nothing more to do with her.

I wondered if that was why she'd gravitated to Roger, a married man who'd obviously lied to her to gain her love. It was a sad situation all around. To break the awkward silence, which was a rarity when you had my family gathered around a table, I asked Jessi if having her party at The Drunken Rooster would be in bad taste. "I know you said earlier you didn't want to go out there when you got out of jail."

She smiled shyly. "I really don't mind. I just didn't want to bring any bad vibes to Genie and Billy Jack's place. If they are fine with having me, I'd love to make a happy memory there. We could have it out back like y'all did with Granny Mack's weddin'. That way, I don't have to linger near the front check-in desk."

"Well now, it sounds like a party is shapin' up. I bet the Shifty River Boys would love to play if Jolene needs us," Uncle Joe said, his grin growing as he glanced at Bonita. My bestie had joined us for dinner and I smiled as she covered his hand with hers.

Aunt Dixie said she would make the birthday cake and Genie volunteered some of the leftover decorations from the wedding. Billy Jack allowed as how he had a raspberry pale ale ready for just such an occasion. "I bet Zeke and Floyd would love to man the barbecue again, too."

Jessi soaked up the love and attention like a sponge and I smiled at her enthusiasm as she interacted with all my family. The only thing missing was Ray. Even though I tried to act like everything was fine, and Uncle Joe and I hadn't told anyone else what had happened to him, I knew we'd have to soon.

Right on cue, Billy Jack questioned the whereabouts of my missing beau. I tried to silence him by glancing at Jessi and raising my eyebrows. She didn't know about Ray. As a mortal, she'd never seen him and wouldn't understand if we told her we were all magickal folks.

Uncle Joe saved the day by elbowing my cousin.

"He's off on an errand for me, son. He'll be back soon."

Aunt Dixie kept the conversation going by asking Jessi what her favorite cake flavor was and whether she wanted one big cake or cupcakes. I breathed a sigh of relief and looked around the table. Bonita held up her pinky and thumb to her ear in the shape of a telephone receiver to show me she wanted to talk later, just me and her. I nodded, relieved that I would be able to share the burden of Ray's disappearance with her.

I was pretty sure Uncle Joe would fill Aunt Dixie in on it too, just so she had a heads up.

I got up and excused myself meaning to go to the restroom and take a breather. The mention of Ray left me needing a moment to myself.

Instead, as I made my way through the diner, I changed my mind and slipped out the front door. A little night air would do me good and I'd have less chance of running into anyone than if I'd gone to the ladies restroom.

Stepping off to the side of the door, where the shadows from the awning over the front of the building were deepest, I distracted myself with people watching and counting cars that drove by. I couldn't begin to think of Ray bound by that nasty goblin. If I went down that road, I'd drive myself crazy. I knew Uncle Joe was working on a plan to draw the woman out and force a fight, but since she had my summoning stone, I was worried about Ray and my connection to him through the stone. We had no way of knowing what might happen.

I was about to go back in when Deputy Carter walked up and tapped me on my shoulder. "Hey Jo, I'm glad I found you out here alone. I've got some news from Cumberland Gap. I'd as soon tell you out here instead of goin' inside and havin' half the town overhear me."

"What's up? Isn't it good news that Jessi's free?"

Deputy Carter glanced down at his boot and scuffed a few rocks on the sidewalk.

"Come on, you know I can handle whatever it is you have to say," I assured him, knowing that it was true, except if he had bad news regarding Ray.

"Well, it seems that Arty somehow escaped from prison and I guess they think Jessi helped him somehow. I have to question her and advise her not to leave Devil's Elbow until they find Arty." He took a deep breath as he looked me in the eye.

Well if that wasn't almost the craziest thing I'd ever heard. I jumped to defend Jessi. "She came to see me before ten this mornin' and she's been in Devil's Elbow ever since. When did Arty bust outta jail and why do they think Jessi was involved?"

"I reckon he was sprung during the lunch hour, and they found a locket with Jessi's name on it in his cell by the door. I know it could be a set-up, and so do they, but I have to do my job, Jolene." He sure didn't sound real happy about it.

I turned and glanced through one of the two front windows of Kudzu's. Jessi was still at the table with my kinfolks, laughing and talking. I hated that I'd have to go in and get her and bring her back out with me, but it was a sight better than having Deputy Carter go in and do it. "Wait here, I'll bring her out to you. I don't want her, or my family, embarrassed in front of half the town. She might put down roots here, someday."

The deputy nodded his understanding. Sighing, I left him standing there rocking on his heels and went back inside. Not wasting time, I asked Jessi to come outside with me. Uncle Joe picked up on my distress. "You okay, short stack? You need my help?"

"I'm fine. I just need to speak with Jessi outside for a minute. We'll be right back." I smiled and hoped he bought it. I didn't want to alert anyone to the fact that a killer had broken out of jail, on top of Jessi being under suspicion of aiding and abetting said murderer, in the middle of a dinner rush at our local cafe.

Jessi held the door for me as I went through and

once we were both outside, I pointed over to where Deputy Carter stood in the shadows. "My friend has some questions for you. I thought it would be better if I brought you out here instead of him walking you out. I'm sorry, Jessi. Arty broke out of jail earlier today."

"Let me guess, they think I helped him?" She didn't miss a beat.

Sighing, I nodded. "Let's go talk to Deputy Carter. He's a family friend and he won't railroad you, I can promise you that."

"But he's got no pull in Cumberland Gap, has he?" Jessie asked.

"I reckon not, but they did ask him to find you and question you so that's something. At least they didn't send him to arrest you right off the bat." I tried to reassure her that things weren't so bad.

By the time Jessi arrived at the police station with Deputy Carter, my family had polished off dessert. After she left Kudzu's in the police cruiser with the deputy, I had moseyed back inside the cafe and told my family that Jessi had gotten an important call and didn't want us to wait on her.

I felt bad not telling the whole truth right then, but once we were all outside in the parking lot after finishing dessert and settling the check with Merlene, I finally spilled the beans. "So, you see, I couldn't tell y'all in there. But the killer is loose again and Jessi might be held here by the police until they find Arty."

Uncle Joe shook his head. "This murder gets weirder and weirder by the day."

Billy Jack crossed his arms and looked at me. "It

surely does. Now, I wanna know what's really goin' on with Ray. I wasn't thinkin' earlier when I asked about him in front of Jessi, but something ain't right."

The time had come to tell them all. "He's been stolen, for lack of a better word, by the goblin. And she sent him to take my summoning stone."

Aunt Dixie put two and two together real quick. "Are you sayin' the goblin has sent Ray around town to steal from all of us?"

"I reckon so. She's gatherin' up things that belong to my magickal friends and family with the goal of forcing me to do her bidding. I don't know why she didn't think kidnapping Ray was enough."

It was the truth. I'd do anything to get Ray back.

My uncle held up a hand and looked around the parking lot to be certain we were all alone. When he was satisfied no one had walked up on us, he put forth his ideas about what the goblin was plotting. "I don't think the plan is to force your hand, Jolene. I think she's after someone else and we better make sure that Sally is safe now that she's back in Devil's Elbow with Freddie."

"What makes you say that, Joe? Freddie and Sally ain't got a thing to do with the murder or the goblin." Aunt Dixie was as confused as I was at first. But then I recalled that Freddie had sent the relic to the Seelie

Queen and that was what the goblin wanted more than anything.

"So the goblin thinks that Freddie will return her necklace if he sees all of us suffering?" I asked Uncle Joe to be certain that was his thinking.

"It makes as much sense as anything else. The only one who could get the queen to give up the relic now would be the elf who possessed it first. If the goblin thinks everything she's done so far won't work, she might set her sights on Sally next." Uncle Joe took his keys from his pocket and jangled them as we all stood thinking.

"Well, they're stayin' out at Red's for the time being. We can go out there," I offered and grabbed the keys from my uncle. "That way you can warn Freddie and stop shadowing me at my place."

"Oh no, short stack. I never said you didn't need my help. That goblin is so unpredictable right now, I wouldn't dare leave your side." Uncle Joe snatched his keys back and I sulked.

He laughed at me and snarked. "You almost had it, short stack. You gotta be quicker than that!"

I gave chase as he turned and dashed towards his truck leaving the rest of our family shaking their heads at our horseplay in the midst of the goblin threat.

The ride out to Maybelle's house, it would always be Maybelle's in my head even though she was no longer among the living, went by with me and Uncle Joe lost in our own thoughts. He knew the twisting roads in these mountains better than just about anybody so being on autopilot worked for both of us.

When we pulled up out front, the lights were still on in the front room and Freddie answered my uncle's knock right away and welcomed us inside. I looked around for Red but only saw Sally. She looked so happy in this domestic setting with Freddie that I hated being the bearer of bad news.

She stood and came to welcome me and Uncle Joe. "It's so good to have you both stop by. I hope nothing's wrong, but by the looks on your faces I think there just might be."

Freddie placed an arm around Sally's shoulders. "Well whatever it is, it can't be worse than that goblin."

Uncle Joe bristled beside me. I felt his energy humming loud enough to beat the band. His words came out in a rush. "Have you seen her? Has she been here?"

I placed a hand on my uncle's arm, hoping to calm him down a little bit.

"Should we have seen her? I've got my elves watching the place and so far, it's been a quiet evening." Freddie didn't seem worried but I was sure our suspicions about Sally would change all that.

"I hope you don't ever see her anywhere near here, but we came to warn y'all that we think she might be after Sally. Or at least something that belongs to her." Uncle Joe still seemed jumpy so I led him to the sofa as I explained to our friends why we thought the way we did.

"Things have been disappearing from friends and family. Small things like a rolling pin and house slippers. And one really big thing, I mean person, or ghost I guess. Ray is under the goblin's spell. We thought she was tryin' to get to me, but since she'd only have to take Ray to make me get her relic back, we think she's actually trying to get to you Freddie. To make you do her bidding to help me and Ray."

My elf friend was confused by the whole convoluted notion. "But why take small things when she really wanted to force my hand? Why not go for Sally right away?"

Uncle Joe chimed in. "We don't know how her mind works. But I do know goblins aren't all that smart. They act mostly from passion. Anger, greed, lust. When you left with Sally and she couldn't find the two of you, since you did usa a spell to cloak yourselves and the relic when you went out Jo's back door, she moved to the next best target in her mind, my niece."

"So now that we're back, you think she'll come for Sally next? I guess that makes sense. I am the only one who could really get the relic back for her," Freddie reasoned as he began to pace the floor in front of the fireplace.

Sally came to sit beside me on the sofa as Uncle Joe stood and joined Freddie by the fireplace. "Jo, why didn't you tell us about Ray when we came over to talk business with you? I can't imagine the worry runnin' through your mind right now."

Grateful for her concern, I rushed to assure her that while I did miss Ray terribly, the goblin couldn't hurt him. "Since he's incorporeal, she can't do much to him except send him around to do her dirty work."

"You've seen him? What happened?" Sally's eyes grew round with wonder.

"It's a long story, but she sent him to steal my summoning stone. I don't know how I'm going to get it back, but I am. And I'm going to bring Ray home too. Nothing will stop me, not even a crazy goblin."

I meant it and of a sudden, my heart lifted. I hadn't felt this hopeful since this whole mess started with the murder of Roger the magician.

I recalled that we were throwing a birthday party

for Jessi and invited Sally and Freddie. "Y'all have to come! It's out at the bed and breakfast tomorrow evening. If Deputy Carter lets Jessi go, I guess."

"Wait, is Jessi out of jail or not? What has Deputy Carter got to do with it?" Sally shrugged. I was good at sowing confusion this evening.

"I'm sorry. In my excitement over Freddie's desire to settle down here in Devil's Elbow, I didn't get to tell y'all that she was let go and that Arty, the magician's manager, broke out of jail. The sheriff over in the Gap thinks Jessi might have sprung him and now Deputy Carter is questioning her and tryin' to figure out what happened. But, before all that, I decided to throw her a party since she spent her birthday locked up."

"I declare Jolene, you do live an excitin' life!" Sally just laughed and shook her head, amazed by the report I'd given her.

I laughed with her. She was right. "I tell you what, Sally, I'm more than ready to be done with all this excitement and try on some boredom for a change."

Uncle Joe came over and grabbed my hand. "Come on short stack. It ain't about to be borin' until we get that goblin sorted and see that Ray Davis is back home where he belongs."

Knowing my uncle was right, I stood and said my goodbyes to Freddie and Sally. I reminded them to take care and added a plea to my elf friend. "She's not to be underestimated, that goblin. If Ray shows up here, don't be mad at him if he does things he normally wouldn't, try to help him Freddie."

"You already know my people are on it, Jo. We'll see that Ray is returned home." His words rang in my ears all the way back to the truck.

Uncle Joe threw it into reverse and I asked him if he knew what the elves of the Seelie Court were up to. He stayed silent on the matter for a mile or so and then answered me all quiet like. "Freddie and I worked out a plan, short stack. If we're real lucky, nobody gets hurt. If we're plumb out of luck, the whole town's in danger. A goblin double crossed is doubly dangerous."

Knowing I'd do whatever was asked of me, I gathered my courage and tapped into my love for Ray. I reached out for him with the ties from my soul to his as our bridge. A warmth flooded my heart in return and even though I couldn't see or hear him, I felt Ray Dang Davis sending me out every ounce of love he had for the fight ahead.

$$18$$

The backyard of The Drunken Rooster was festooned with dozens of peach and light green helium balloons. Mrs. Davis had donated them from her flower shop along with a large bouquet of carnations for the birthday girl.

She'd been fit to be tied to hear about Ray but she didn't hold Jessi responsible for the mess. The fact that Uncle Joe promised to bring her son home went a long way in soothing my future mother-in-law.

Her words came back to me as I watched her move about the tables making sure everything was just right. She'd hugged my uncle there in her flower shop as she organized the party balloons earlier in the day. "I've known y'all my whole life and I know you're good people. If anyone can help my son, it's Joe Mack."

Jessi had been put on notice by Deputy Carter that she had to remain in Devil's Elbow, but since she'd made great friends of Aunt Dixie and myself, we'd begged him to let her leave city limits to go over to Cumberland Gap for her birthday celebration. I'd reasoned with him that she hadn't run from anyone and that she would be with all of us. That included him as he was given an invitation to come along, and not just as law enforcement.

Uncle Joe had filled him in on the goblin's thievery and what we all thought she meant by it. Since he was family, he'd decided on his own that we needed his help as much as he needed ours.

Tonight, I wanted to push away thoughts of the goblin at least long enough to enjoy the party. Breathing in the aroma of barbecue that wafted across the yard, I felt my tastebuds water. My feet vetoed any other plans I may have had and took me straight to the tables of food set out for the birthday dinner.

Floyd swatted my hand away from the basket of corn fritters and only relented after I promised him I'd supply him with my last few jars of Billy Jack's last moonshine batch. "I ain't got no use for it other than trading it for favors, but I reckon if you give me this basket of corn fritters, it's a fair trade."

Zeke shook his head. "That ain't fair a'tall and he

knows it! Take them fritters on the house, Jolene. We've got more on that other table over there."

I held up my hand and bargained Floyd down to one jar for the basket of fritters. Zeke shook his head as he walked off mumbling about how some folks don't know how to leave well enough alone. Laughing, I took off with my tasty treasure.

This was just the kind of thing I needed, friends and family acting like everything was normal. It was that type of evening I wanted to lose myself in before we had to gird our loins for the fight against the goblin.

Freddie and Uncle Joe had their plan, but they hadn't breathed another word of it to any of us and I decided that this fight belonged to all of us, and I wasn't alone in it. Even though I knew we'd be better with Granny at our backs, this fight wasn't hers. But what a story we'd have for her and Mr. B when they got home from their honeymoon!

Walking around the backyard alone, I took in the music, dancing, and merriment with a tiny pain in my heart. Ray would be back with me soon and we'd have a celebration like this on our wedding night. I wondered if he'd want to do it here or someplace else, like his mama's house. Her backyard would be perfect.

Bonita touched my arm and I reluctantly left my

dream world. "You alright, sugar? You looked so lonesome over here, I had to come and see about you."

Her sweet smile and the concern in her eyes snapped me out of my melancholy mood. "I'm fine as frog hair split three ways, girlfriend. I was just thinkin' about the future."

"I was thinkin' the same. Watchin' your granny tie the know with Mr. B and hearing that Genie and Billy Jack are planning their vows, well, it gets you to thinkin', you know?" She was baring her soul to me and I resisted the urge to talk about myself.

"Are you thinkin' about becoming a Mack? Because if you are, that would make me happier than a fat old toad on a lily pad. You think my uncle is about to pop the question?" My voice lowered as I grilled her. I didn't want anyone else to overhear our private conversation.

Bonita shrugged but she wasn't upset. "I don't know. He acts so lovey dovey when we're alone, but lately he's been preoccupied. I guess this business with the murder and the goblin has him on edge. Can't say I blame him."

"I think he feels responsible for everything. Since Granny is gone, the pressure is on him to make sure we're all fine. That's why he's been camped out at my apartment. I've tried to send him away, but there's no way he'd go with danger lurking."

She fairly beamed with pride. "And that's why I love him."

The silence following her heartfelt declaration stretched between us for a long minute.

"Did you just say what I think you said? You love my uncle?" I touched her arm gently and tried to hide the smile that played on my lips.

"I do. I did. I mean, he's amazing Jolene. I tried to deny it. I told myself it was wrong to fall for my best friend's uncle, but you know what? I couldn't make my heart stop singing whenever he was near. That's never happened with anyone before. I mean I've liked other men, even admired a few of them. But love? Not before Joe Mack."

Her testimony there in the backyard under the stars was a beautiful thing and I swallowed the lump in my throat. Happy that my uncle had a good woman who truly loved him and that Bonita most definitely had him, I hugged her tight around the neck. "Well, if you need a blessing, you've surely got mine. I couldn't think of a better woman for him than you, sweet friend."

We laughed and talked for another few minutes before I followed her to the dance floor. Just us girl-friends dancing together. PJ left her seat with enthu-siasm and joined us. We were three young witches again dancing together in the moonlight in the middle of someone else's party.

The music stopped abruptly and Uncle Joe dropped his guitar as Freddie moved toward the far edge of the dance floor. Jessi cried out in frustration. "Why won't you leave me alone? I can't help you!"

I rushed forward with Bonita and PJ at my back. The sight of Arty stopped me in my tracks. He was pale, obviously in pain, and he held out one hand as he staggered toward Jessi on the dance floor. With the darkened woods behind him, he was a scary sight.

"You don't understand Jessi! You HAVE to get that relic back! She's gonna kill everybody in her path if your friends don't help us!" He pleaded on and on, his voice rising as he came closer and closer.

Uncle Joe warned him to stay back. "I don't know what that goblin's done to you, but you stay where you are, man. I'd rather not hurt you but I will."

The power surging through my uncle sparked in the fingertips of his outstretched hand. If Arty didn't heed that warning, he was truly mad.

Jessi left the circle that me, Bonita, and PJ had made around her and moved toward Arty. Freddie did not like that move one bit. "Jessi, something's wrong with him. Don't get too close."

Deputy Carter appeared in a flash and took hold

of Jessi's arm. "You're my responsibility and he's an escaped felon. Did you know he'd be here tonight?"

Jessi's vehement denial cheered me, but this party was headed in the wrong direction. Thankful the deputy had been able to halt her progress toward Arty, I took a moment to scan the perimeter of the yard. I saw Billy Jack doing the same and we nodded when our eyes met.

I went to Genie and moved her and Mrs. Davis to the middle of the yard, as far from trouble as possible. "No matter what happens, you two stay here, okay? Things could get ugly if Arty doesn't stand down."

Genie understood perfectly, she'd seen the supernatural fracas in Louisville at the baking contest.

Satisfied that I'd moved them away from the trouble, I rejoined my friends. Aunt Dixie moved back closer to Genie and Mrs. Davis and took Sally with her. Freddie and Uncle Joe were joined by Billy Jack and I took my girlfriends and brought up the rear forming a line behind Genie and her mama to protect our flank.

A breeze picked up and whistled through the trees and I shivered. That wind was cold, not the warm breeze of a summer night. Someone else had come to join Arty in his bid to pry the relic from

Freddie, but as far as I knew, the Seelie Queen still had the object.

I looked to my girlfriends and we all called up our mountain witch powers to form a crackling line of protection behind those we loved.

Craning my neck, I tried to see Arty and listen for Uncle Joe or Freddie to tell us what was going on. Instead, the attack came at our rear and I was glad I'd placed myself in the direct line of fire.

The goblin had shed all attempts to appear as a human female and her true form was horrible to behold. Thick, scaly dark green skin like a dragon covered her and her eyes glowed red. There were fangs protruding over her rubbery lips and drool dripped from them unheeded. Fear would have over-taken me, but I saw Ray at her side and anger rose hot and quick to replace it.

"Let him go and you can deal with my elf friend for the relic you seek. As long as you hold Ray Davis captive, you'll never have what you want most, I assure you." I spoke calmly to the beastly thing.

She stretched out a clawed hand and shot a stream of magick my way that caused such pain it nearly took me clean to my knees. Bonita and PJ had thrown up a shield around me and it blunted the power of the first attack.

Sweat rolled off me and I gritted my teeth to keep

my sanity. Uncle Joe pulled me back behind him and the pain lessened a considerable bit. That meant he was now taking the brunt of it.

With a loud grunt that showed how deeply my uncle dug into his power, he unleashed his own boundless magick at the goblin. Uncle Joe's attack would have felled any other magickal creature, but the goblin was equal to the challenge.

Gathering my wits, I turned and instructed Bonita and PJ to gather up the mortals and herd them inside the house. "Protect them no matter what happens here. Understood?"

My girls moved like lightning to make sure Genie and Jessi and the others, including poor Arty and Mrs. Davis and Sally, were safely away from the battle. I saw Deputy Carter secure the French doors and post up in front of them on the deck as another line of defense.

For those of us who were magickal beings, the worst outcome would be if mortals were injured in the midst of a battle that had very little to do with them.

Secure in the knowledge that the weakest among us were out of the way, I searched the darkness for Billy Jack. We came together behind Uncle Joe and then split off to his left and right to attack the goblin's flanks.

Ray called out to me, and I inched closer and closer to the goblin hoping to find a way to help him. His voice carried across the whipping winds and I knew he wanted me to stay back and let my uncle and cousin do the fighting.

Instead, I kept up my attack while steadily gaining ground toward my objective. Freddie came to my side swiftly, with his hand out and a goofy grin on his face. When he opened his hand, there was my summoning stone!

"How on earth?" I yelled but he shook his head and shoved the stone into my hand.

"Take it, she's got a fake. You didn't think I'd let her get the real thing did you? Before I left for Pigeon Forge, I replaced your stone with one very similar but as useless as a lump of coal."

I wanted to laugh and hug him and dance around with glee, but all that would come later. Now I had to focus all my energy into the stone in order to weaken the goblin.

Power surged through me and into the stone, swirling within its smooth surface and then pouring back into me, the magick amplified beyond even my wildest imagination.

When I whispered a spell I hoped would sever Ray from her side and end her control over him, the beast whirled on me, her frustrated shrieks filling the world around me. Instead of stepping back, I pushed forward chanting Ray's name over and over, stretching my soul towards his while holding firm inside my body.

The stone wanted the essential part of me, my soul, to pull free and fly to Ray but I knew if I did, the goblin would then control me. I couldn't risk that.

Uncle Joe and Billy Jack took over the attack on her flank while I dueled with the goblin for Ray. She was weakening when I sent the strongest pulse of magick straight to where I thought her heart might be, if she had one.

In a crazy moment where the wind died down and her shrieks were silenced, Ray came to me, happy tears flowing freely down his ghostly face. "Jo! I knew you would come for me! I'm so proud of you, baby!"

He hugged me tight, careful not to cross before the magick that poured forth from my hands. Feeling the warmth of his form behind me as he moved back to support me, I felt my magick was winning over the goblin.

I should have known fighting that ugly beast wouldn't be that easy. She rose back up, her fury at the severance of Ray from her side fueling her anger.

With one sweep of her scaly hand, I fell backward onto my rear end, my stone clutched in my hand and

Ray hovering in front of me to block her way. When she shot out another one of her darts of pain, my boyfriend blocked it with a ninja move that had my eyes nearly popping out in surprise. I laughed at the absurdity of it and it took me several minutes to realize that Ray was effectively shielding me. Something was very wrong, or very right depending on how you looked at it.

When Ray couldn't hold her back any longer, I hopped up and dusted myself off. I'd worn my favorite sundress for the birthday party and it didn't look like I'd ever wear it again. There were wisps of smoke lifting off me here and there and the hem was tattered and singed. Dang it all!

Ready to battle the beast again, I called up my magick again. My summoning stone was safely tucked into my right hand and I felt its comforting weight, light and solid though it was, and enjoyed the thrill of my magick moving through my limbs.

Billy Jack had shifted to his wolf and Uncle Joe wasn't far behind. That meant the goblin was lumbering my way. The vibration of the earth as she moved proved my intuition correct.

Ray stood beside me as I squared up to deliver the most powerful blast I could muster. It hit her full force and sent her spinning backward so fast, Billy Jack barely had time to leap out of the way. If he hadn't been in his wolf form, I don't think he could have done it.

In the blink of an eye, the backyard was filled with elves. Freddie led the charge and they descended on the goblin.

My family kept the perimeter secure while the army of the Seelie Queen made short work of the beast. What was left of her was carted off in a large truck they'd brought just for that purpose. When they were gone and the area was cleared by Uncle Joe and Billy Jack, Deputy Carter cuffed Arty and warned Jessi that he'd be back for her. "I reckon your birthday is ruined, but I'll let y'all have some sort of celebration since the goblin is routed."

He tipped his hat and was gone before I could speak to him. I wanted him to know how much we appreciated him protecting our loved ones. I knew how hard it was for him to hold back and watch such a battle without joining in with us. The lawman side and the warlock in him had likely strained to be unleashed into the fight.

Ray grabbed me up in a hug and passed through me several times in an attempt to make me feel his love. It was like old times when he used to pass through me to see how I was feeling about things. I hoped he could tell loud and clear how happy I was to see him again, to have him so near and safe from harm.

"I feel it, Jo. Your love had kept me sane through all this madness. Our soul connection gave me the strength to hold her off there at the last after she knocked you down. I was able to protect you the way you protected me. Isn't it a miracle?"

He was so excited, so happy, that I couldn't think of anything more than how perfect we were for each other. No matter what form either of us took, we would always love each other. I punched his shoulder hard. My fear finally surfaced. "Don't ever do that again Ray Dang Davis!"

Bless his heart, he immediately went from giddy with love to sorrowful over what we'd both been through. "I won't Jo, never again. I didn't know anyone could bind a ghost like she did but now that I do, you and I have to figure out a way to keep that from ever happening again, okay?"

His pleas for my help melted my heart and I pulled him into my arms and tiptoed to kiss his pale lips. "Never losing you again, my love. It would be the end of me."

When he finally let go, I couldn't help all the questions that tumbled from my lips. The most important one was about Arty. "He really did kill Roger?

Ray nodded. "The goblin had come to town to find the relic her husband took from her. The poor fool hadn't known his wife was a magickal creature. Which is ironic when you think about it. But anyway, he meant to sell it and Arty was trying to stop him. The goblin showed up and handed him the knife that ended Roger's life. The way Arty told it to me was that he had no choice. He owed the goblin allegiance or some such nonsense."

"So when she broke him out of jail, she tried to make it look like Jessi had a part in that? What a mess! But it's over now, at least for us. I don't ever want to see a goblin again, not even at Halloween. That thing nearly scared me to death!" It was true and I trembled a little as Ray held me close.

"You were so brave, Jo. I know how hard it was to hold it together once you found out what happened, but you did it. You're made of steel, woman." His kisses along my jaw and down my neck felt like butterfly wings.

The rest of my family was busy cleaning up the backyard and trying to restore some semblance of a celebration. Ray tried to pull me away and into the house but I knew we had to help everyone get through the effects of adrenaline and magick. We all needed a ton of food and gallons of Genie's tea or, better yet, Billy Jack's legal brew.

"We can have a proper reunion later, at home where we belong. Delilah will be wild with joy when she sees you. We have a long night ahead, my love. Can you manage it after holding back a goblin?"

He laughed and ran a hand through my hair lifting the locks to catch the scent of my shampoo. I didn't know how he could smell anything other than smoke, but he inhaled deeply and grinned. "After that performance, you ought to know better than to ask me that Jolene. You're in for the time of your life, woman."

I tilted my head to the side and tried to look serious. "Maybe I'm the one who can't handle any more excitement tonight?"

Ray goosed my ribs and I squealed. Running off into the dark fields beyond the backyard, I hoped he caught me and showed me again how deep was our love.

The End

ALSO BY ELLIE MOSES

The Hillbilly Hexes Series

Moonshine and Manslaughter

Huckleberries and Homicide

The Kudzu Killer

The Abracadabra Cadaver

Novellas in Hillybilly Hexes series:

Happy Hexmas (Christmas novella)

Peril in the Pumpkin Patch (Halloween novella available for newsletter subscribers only. Get it here!)

ABOUT THE AUTHOR

Ellie Moses loves magic and mystery and hails from the hills and hollows of Appalachia. Her favorite TV shows growing up were The Beverly Hillbillies and Bewitched. It's no wonder she aims to keep the fun and magic of those two childhood favorites alive in her Hillbilly Hexes cozy mystery series.

Contact Ellie on her Facebook page using the icon below or email her at authorelliemoses@gmail.com. Her website is elliemoses.com and you may sign up for her newsletter here for news and your copy of *Peril in the Pumpkin Patch*. To join her reader group on Facebook, follow this link: https://www.facebook.com/groups/2487426861547026 Be sure to follow her on Amazon too!

www.ingramcontent.com/pod-product-compliance
Lightning Source LLC
Chambersburg PA
CBHW031301160726
47993CB00001B/258